aunty lee's delights

aunty lee's delights

OVIDIA YU

WILLIAM MORROW
An Imprint of HarperCollins*Publishers*

P.S.™ is a trademark of HarperCollins Publishers.

HarperCollins books may be purchased for educational, business, or sales promotional use. For information please e-mail the Special Markets Department at SPsales@harpercollins.com.

FIRST EDITION

Designed by Diahann Sturge

Library of Congress Cataloging-in-Publication Data has been applied for.

ISBN 978-0-06-222715-7

13 14 15 16 17 OV/RRD 10 9 8 7 6 5 4 3 2 1

In loving memory of Christina Sergeant
(1955–2013)

aunty lee's delights

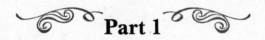

Part 1

Introducing Death and Detectives

Prologue

First Body

It was early morning and the rain had stopped. The grass was still wet. They walked across it to the sand and then right up to the water's edge. The beach was not private to the hotel but there was no one else there at that hour. The combination of dawn and low-tide debris gave the impression of old secrets washed up, ready to be revealed. A light breeze came across the water, bringing the smell of salt and distant decay as well as—this being Singapore— whiffs of industrial chemicals being fired and antimosquito fogging.

Tired as they were, being so close to the water cast its spell on them. Even if the sea before them was blocked from the ocean by Indonesia and East Malaysia and crowded with tankers and cruisers, it was still a boundary and a reminder that somewhere in the beyond surrounding them there was a vital ocean and living planet. Like many other city- and computer-bound people, the two were unfamiliar with the experience of being exposed to the wind, the waves, and physical space.

Holding hands and their footwear, they walked barefoot along the shoreline talking about the past and their future. They were not yet twenty-four hours into their newborn marriage and found it fascinating. The Sentosa beach might have been artificially constructed but it was all the more romantic for that, with the best-quality, daily swept sand and line of carefully placed shallow rock pools marking low-tide boundaries.

"Look, a hermit crab!"

"I already noticed you in Junior College, you know . . ."

"I noticed you before that. Why do you think I decided to go to Anglo-Chinese Junior College with Hwa Chong at my door step? My parents thought I was crazy!"

"Do you think we'll ever be here like this again?"

"We can come back every year if you like. Every anniversary."

"It won't be the same. You'll be playing golf and busy and maybe there'll be children—I mean, maybe not but—" She broke off awkwardly, embarrassed to have mentioned children. But he was equal to the subject.

"Of course there'll be children. Lots of children. Your

parents and my parents can fight over who gets to look after them, but once a year, every year, we'll come back here, just the two of us, okay?"

"There's something over there!" she said then, squinting over the beach. It was the most romantic thing he had ever said and she did not want to spoil it just yet by pointing out that she expected anniversary trips far further abroad—Europe, or America, maybe. "Over there. It looks like a jellyfish; is it? It's huge!"

"It's not a jellyfish. It's just a plastic bag . . ."

"Yes, it's a jellyfish—I can see its body and its legs and everything. Can't you see? I think it's dead. Are there poisonous jellyfish around Sentosa?"

They smelled it before they saw it was no jellyfish.

She screamed. He was sick on the sand. Then they put on their gritty sandals and ran back to the hotel to call the police.

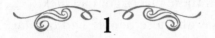

1

Aunty Lee's Delights

"Now they are finding bodies on the beach! I tell you, that place is bad luck! Do you know it used to be called Pulau Blakang Mati? That means 'Island of Death.' Before your time, of course, but everybody in Singapore will remember. Crazy, right? Go and build a tourist resort in a place called Island of Death."

"But now it is called Sentosa, right? And the meaning of Sentosa is 'happy peacefulness'?" Nina kept her eyes focused on her work. Now she was efficiently threading thin, diagonally cut slices of chicken thigh meat onto bamboo skewers, pressing them well together before returning them to their marinade.

"So? They can call it whatever they want—they still found a dead body there, true or not?"

"Ma'am, they also find dead body in the HDB water tank, in the Singapore River, in Serangoon Reservoir. You cannot say all these places got bad luck."

"I would say all those people had bad luck. But at least we know who they were, right? This one is supposed to be unidentified!"

News that an unidentified woman's body had been found washed up on a Sentosa beach in a plastic bag had not made it into any of the Singapore morning papers, but it had been the hottest news online and over the radio all day. For once, the radio in Aunty Lee's Delights had been turned on all day, switching between local stations for updates.

Aunty Lee's Delights was a small café shop in Binjai Park, less than five minutes' walk from Dunearn Road. It was well-known for good traditional Peranakan food and famous for the *achar* and sambals Aunty Lee had been selling out of her house for years. Aunty Lee's Delights was also equipped with the latest modern equipment. Though she was revered for cooking the traditional standards, strange dishes occasionally popped up because Aunty Lee loved experimenting. In her view, anything cooked with local ingredients was local food. In fact the shop was very like Aunty Lee herself. Another passion of hers was reverse engineering dishes (and occasionally people) to figure out how they had come about and how they might be better adjusted. She called her kitchen her laboratory for DIY-*CSI*, the television in there testifying to her two passions, for food and news.

Aunty Lee was a short, precise Peranakan lady of certain age and even more certain girth. The image of her fair, plump, *kebaya*-clad form smiling on jars of Aunty Lee's Amazing Achar and Aunty Lee's Shiok Sambal was familiar to most Singaporeans and probably anyone else who had been on the island for any extended length of time. Today Aunty Lee was wearing a turquoise *kebaya* top with matching pants so flared that she looked like she was wearing a skirt when not in motion. Her sneakers that afternoon were turquoise with bright yellow laces. Aunty Lee believed in tradition but even more in comfort.

Aunty Lee was also well-known and a bit of a headache to many of the island city's food suppliers. Through letters to the *Straits Times*, she had exposed several cases of food fraud ("organic" *kailan* that had been sprayed with insecticide, "free-range" chicken with the flaccid thigh meat of cage-bound animals). All thanks to her unerring ability to pinpoint when something was "off," in food or in life, and being *kiasu* enough to fixate on it. *Kiasu*, or fear of losing out, was a typical Singaporean characteristic and one that Aunty Lee embodied to the extreme.

All day Aunty Lee had been following news reports on radio and television and had even sent Nina round to the 7-Eleven to pick up the afternoon papers, but she hadn't learned any more about the body that had been found.

She and Nina had overdosed on DJ chatter and music (which Nina had quite enjoyed when Aunty Lee was not changing channels hoping for more news), but all she had gotten were news updates without new information and speculations from phone-in callers. Was it the body of a gambler from the casino? An illegal immigrant dropped off a boat who had failed to swim in to shore? Or an unlucky sailor? Had it been an accident, a suicide, or—most exciting of all—murder?

Naturally Aunty Lee was all in favor of suicide or murder. She did not find accidents very interesting. To her, accidents were the result of carelessness and poor planning, and she had very little interest in or patience with careless and lazy people. She found them boring.

"They should let us know what is happening!" Aunty Lee said. "How can they keep people in the dark like that. It's not as though they are preparing for an election or something—a body on Sentosa is serious, it affects all of us. What if tourists start to worry and stop going to the Integrated Resort there to gamble? It's going to affect all of us!"

"They can also go to the other resort to gamble, ma'am," Nina said practically. Very little upset Nina Balignasay. "Anyway, nowadays they find dead bodies in Singapore quite often."

"Do you think they've found any more bodies? Turn on the TV again. Go to CNN. Sometimes, if it's big enough, Singapore news comes out there before it reaches Singapore."

"If they find more bodies, then it is more likely accident, ma'am. Maybe it is a boat sinking."

"Or a mass murder!" Aunty Lee said with relish. "One of those serial killers. After all, if you are going to go through all the trouble of arranging to throw somebody into the sea, why stop at one body, right?"

As she spoke, Aunty Lee was rapidly cutting up cucumbers with all the attention she normally paid to cooking, which was not much. She cooked the way some people drove—while carrying on conversations, applying lipstick, and texting messages—trusting the instinct that came with long practice and only focusing on the main task when something unexpected came up or went wrong.

Fortunately Aunty Lee did not drive.

"Who do you think it was? The news said unidentified female body. That means nobody reported her missing, right? What kind of relatives don't report a missing girl!"

"Her relatives may not know she's missing yet," Nina observed calmly.

In many ways Nina Balignasay was the opposite of Aunty Lee. Nina was slim, dark, and generally prided herself on minding her own business. Though she had not known how to cook or drive when she arrived in Singapore, she had since learned to do both proficiently, thanks to Aunty Lee's help-others-to-become-good-at-helping-me philosophy. And since keeping Aunty Lee comfortable was her main business, Nina's own powers of observation had also sharpened considerably.

She had also learned not to worry that her employer would lose a finger or an eye as she speed-sliced and waved her knife around to emphasize whatever point she was making. After all, Nina was nothing if not adaptable. She had been trained as a nurse in the Philippines (even if her nursing degree was not recognized in Singapore) and would have been able to stanch the bleeding. And she had learned it was dangerous—and pretty much impossible—to try to stop Aunty Lee from doing what she wanted to.

"You think so? How can relatives not know?"

"How often do you see your relatives, ma'am?"

Aunty Lee paused in thought. Though equipped with an extensive social network, she had few close relatives left alive.

"Call Mark," she said to Nina. "Call Mark and ask him whether that wife of his is around."

Mark Lee was the son of Aunty Lee's late husband and his first wife. Aunty Lee had gotten along fairly well with both M. L. Lee's children for years. Mark was already studying in Australia and Mathilda in the UK when their widower father finally remarried, and they had appreciated the energy Aunty Lee brought into their father's home and life even if the richness of her cooking gave him gout in two years. As Mathilda said, their mother had been dead for over fifteen years, so neither she herself nor Mark had showed any antagonism toward the plump, fair "aunty" who began appearing by their father's side at family and social functions. Indeed, when M. L. Lee married Rosie

Gan, as Aunty Lee had been called before the marriage, his two children had congratulated themselves that there would now be someone to keep their father fed and occupied, thus freeing them to focus on their own families. "We don't have to feel bad about not staying in Singapore to keep an eye on poor old Pa!" as Mathilda said.

Mathilda had married an Englishman and settled in Warwick not long after the wedding, comfortably assured that her father was taken care of. However, things had changed after Mark married and M. L. Lee died of a heart attack—unrelated events that had taken place in the same month almost five years ago. Mrs. Selina Lee had never forgiven her late father-in-law for interrupting her Italian honeymoon by dying (they had been in the Prada café in Montevarchi waiting for her turn to enter the factory outlet when they got the news of his death) or for leaving all his earthly possessions to his second wife.

Aunty Lee privately believed that if Mark had married anyone other than Selina, M. L. Lee would probably have left a great deal more to his son than he did. The late M. L. Lee had had a bias against women with loud shrill voices like his new daughter-in-law. This was perhaps unfair to Selina, who had been deliberately louder (and shriller) in M. L. Lee's presence since his habit of not answering her convinced her that the old man was going deaf. Selina Lee was also convinced that Aunty Lee had stolen her Mark's inheritance from him. Aunty Lee knew that Selina had already been to two different law firms to try to find someone willing to help her contest the will. Aunty Lee might have told Mark that she would leave M. L. Lee's property to him and Selina, which would have made things much more peaceful, but she had not. Instead, she had already agreed to make several loans, of considerable amounts of money, as requested, which Selina now referred to as "presents" and which Mark had already lost in previous business ventures. Running a wine import business was his latest attempt at entrepreneurship.

"What do you want to say to Ma'am Selina?" Nina continued with what she was doing, making no move toward the phone.

"I don't want to talk to that Silly-Nah. I just want to make sure she's still alive. You are the one who said I don't know whether my relatives are missing or not!"

"I never say that, ma'am. Anyway, they will be coming here soon. And if Ma'am Selina is missing, Sir Mark will call the police, right?"

"Who knows?" Aunty Lee grouched. "If she's not there to tell him how to pick up the phone and how to dial, you think he'll know how to do it?"

But she left the subject. Of course, Aunty Lee would have done everything in her power to comfort her stepson if it turned out to be his wife's body that had just floated up onto that Sentosa beach. Aunty Lee would probably miss poor dead Selina, if such were the case—Selina made life more interesting, in the same way as *chili padi* spiced up a dish. But it was all wishful thinking. Selina, very much alive and still bossy, would soon arrive with Mark for that evening's wine dining event.

It was the dining portion of that evening's wine dining that Aunty Lee and Nina were currently preparing. Usually dinner was not served at Aunty Lee's Delights. The café specialized in lunches with an all-day snacks and tea menu that covered everything from late breakfasts to high tea, but it closed at six to allow Aunty Lee to get home for her own dinner. In the old days, dinner had been prepared throughout the day in the shop kitchen and collected, along with herself, by M. L. Lee on his way home from work. M. L. Lee had worked right up to the day of his death. Their Binjai Park bungalow, deeper in the estate, was a fifteen-minute walk from the shop. But even a fifteen-minute walk was not easy in the Singapore evening heat, especially with *tingkats* full of dinner.

Aunty Lee had not realized how much she missed cooking those dinners till the wine dining sessions began. Serving Aunty Lee's local Peranakan dishes accompanied by fine wines chosen by Mark had been Selina Lee's idea. But in spite of this, Aunty Lee enjoyed them very much indeed. She had cut herself off from social life after her husband's death, preferring to cook small dishes rather than make small talk. But she was looking forward to tonight's session; with an unidentified body, there would be more than small talk around the table.

"It could be some foreign diplomat got drunk and ran over somebody then dumped her body into the sea," Aunty

Lee mused. "Do you know if the Romanian embassy sent over a new guy yet?"

"Even if the newspapers say 'unidentified,' it could mean that the police know but didn't tell them, right?" Nina suggested calmly. "Maybe they want to inform the family first."

"Maybe." Undeterred, Aunty Lee branched off on a new track. "And now also, just before Chinese New Year—must be somebody on drugs or on holiday . . . that's why nobody reported her missing yet. They didn't say where this woman is from, right? Tell you what, Nina. Go and phone them and ask whether it is somebody you know. Tell them a friend of yours is missing, then maybe they will tell you whether the woman is Chinese or Indian or *ang moh* . . . but make sure you sound upset, otherwise they will want to get information from you instead . . . Phone now before people start coming for the dinner."

"Ma'am. My hands are dirty now. And I got to finish making dinner before the people come."

"Maybe she went to Sentosa to gamble and lost all her money and she was running away from loan sharks and fell into the sea . . ."

"Yes, ma'am. Do you want me to put the pork on the sticks also?"

"Yes, Nina. Are there enough sticks? Good. Those loan sharks can be so terrible. But they should realize that if they go around killing people, they won't get their money back, right? Unless, of course, they killed her as a warning to other people who owe them money. But if I were a loan shark, I wouldn't kill somebody who really owed me money—I would pick somebody who didn't and just tell everybody she did. That would be enough to frighten them. So that poor girl could be a total stranger to them . . . but maybe it wasn't loan sharks at all. Maybe it was those expat traders who get drunk and beat up taxi drivers. Maybe it was a female taxi driver and she jumped into the sea to get away from them."

Aunty Lee was happy again, Nina thought. Aunty Lee was usually happy when she cooked, but today, despite the frustration of having no details about the body found, she was even happier than usual. Aunty Lee was bored, Nina realized. It was to occupy her mind that she had thrown herself into Aunty Lee's Delights after her husband died. Running the café and keeping the shop counter stocked up with Aunty Lee's "specials" had succeeded in distracting her for a while, but now that routines were established and running smoothly, Aunty Lee was clearly getting bored. Boredom was all very well. Everyone felt bored at times. But a mind that worked with the speed of Aunty Lee's meant boredom would be followed very soon by action and change.

Nina sighed inwardly; she did not want things to change. She was very happy working for Aunty Lee. There were far worse employers to work for. Nina knew that very well, having worked for some of them herself. And it had been Aunty Lee who rescued her, offering to take over her employment contract. "I could report them for what they did to you, of course. But then such things take a long time to get to court and then you won't be able to work or go home—why don't you come and work for me?" It had worked out for both Aunty Lee and Nina . . . and for Nina's former employers, who escaped being fined and blacklisted by maid agencies.

The menu for that night's wine dining gathering was chicken and pork satay, *luak chye* (mustard greens that had been pickling in vinegar, ginger, and sugar since yesterday—Nina had only to remember to mix in the mustard powder just before serving . . .), and the *hee peow* or fish maw soup made with prawn, fish, and meatballs. Of course the whole point of the wine dining dinners were for Aunty Lee's stepson, Mark, to introduce people to wines that could "go" with local food, but Aunty Lee had gleefully seized the opportunity to fire up her favorite recipes. Most visitors who came to Aunty Lee's Delights were there to shop for her sweet and savory *kueh*, fried delicacies, and, of course, the bottles of Aunty Lee's Shiok Sambal and Aunty Lee's Amazing Achar and Krunchy Kropok, which sold out as fast as Aunty Lee and Nina could produce them.

Aunty Lee's hand phone rang. It was on the counter and Nina, correctly interpreting Aunty Lee's "On it for me—make it loud-loud!," answered and switched it to speakerphone.

"Rosie, ah—are you there? Busy or not—" Nina recognized the grainy voice of Mrs. AwYong, an old friend of Aunty Lee's.

"Jin, how are you? Cooking lah. What's up?"

"Rosie, you were right! I found my watch—some more I found an earring and a part of a necklace and a bangle I didn't even know were missing!"

"I told you I was right!" Aunty Lee smirked. Nina smiled to herself. Aunty Lee knew she was usually right but she never tired of hearing others admit it. She grumbled (at least on the surface) when her friends jokingly gave her their challenging little problems to solve to "keep her brain active," but the truth was she adored them. These little problems were a legitimate way of putting what the late M. L. Lee described as his wife's outstanding talent for being "*kiasu, kaypoh, em zhai se!*" Nina could remember the old man saying *kaypoh*, meaning minding the business of others with as much energy as *kiasu* devoted to their own. *Em zhai se* literally meant "not scared to die" and effectively described how Aunty Lee drove everyone around her to despair through frustration as she pursued some triviality no one else could see any point in.

It was a good thing old Uncle Lee had been so fond of his little wife. Where any other man would probably have been irritated, M. L. Lee had been entertained. But then Aunty Lee, with her knack for understanding people (through the way they eat, she said), had probably known him better than anyone else. Nina guessed that

Aunty Lee had seen he needed someone. That would go some way to explaining why she had chosen to marry a man so much older than she was. Because despite what people whispered, and what M. L. Lee's daughter-in-law frequently said aloud, Aunty Lee had had money of her own when she married her widower. Not as much as he had, of course. Few people in Singapore belonged in his class. But after years of catering for special events, Aunty Lee had been comfortable financially and her prowess in the kitchen was unchallenged. What woman could ask for more? Watching Aunty Lee now, Nina wished she knew.

"They were all in the bushes!" The voice coming through the phone shrieked with laughter. "I was so sure the maid took my watch—I even scolded her already—and all along it was the stupid dog! He was taking all my things out to chew. Now all so dirty and smelly already! Hey, did you hear about the dead woman they found on Sentosa? Must be somebody murdered their maid and tried to hide the body, that's why not reported missing!"

"Jin, you imagine such crazy things! I hope it's not your maid that they found there!"

Aunty Lee said little more, ending the call soon after that. Nina knew her well enough to guess her boss was turning over Mrs. AwYong's suggestion. And probably wishing she had thought of it herself.

"That woman always blames the maid first," she said to Nina. "Lost her things, blame the maid. Unidentified body found, must be the maid."

There was a note of apology in Aunty Lee's voice for Mrs. AwYong. But Nina knew only too well that most employers in Singapore regarded their live-in domestic help with great suspicion. That was another reason Nina constantly reminded herself how lucky she was to work for Aunty Lee.

"Did you taste the satay sauce yet?" Nina reminded her boss. Though Nina did most of the food preparation now, Aunty Lee still calibrated the final seasonings.

Aunty Lee moved across to taste the peanut sauce again. It was in the sauces and seasonings, as she constantly reminded Nina, that the real art of cooking was to be found. And it was no use asking for exact measurements either. There were no exact measurements; it was more a matter of training your taste to recognize the perfect pitch so that you could always rely on yourself to adjust the ingredients to hit precisely the right note. What good were recipes that gave you pounds and ounces—or worse, grams and liters—when how much a dish required depended on the quality and age of your ingredients?

Nina watched as Aunty Lee added a dash of coriander and a spoonful of tamarind pulp before giving the sauce a good stir. Selina had tried to suggest that Aunty Lee serve up more bland dishes, ones less likely to overwhelm the wines that were, after all, the whole point of the exercise. Aunty Lee had pointed out that true Peranakan food was always spicy—and suggested Selina phone in an order for delivery pizzas instead—with all the earnest, bland helpfulness of an old lady who was only trying to be helpful . . .

"They should be here soon," Nina said. "Shall I set the table first or wait for Sir Mark?"

"Put out the plates but not the glasses. He'll want to fuss with the glasses himself like he always does. I'm surprised he isn't here already, to let his wine 'settle and breathe' and whatever nonsense." Aunty Lee brightened. "Maybe he's late because that Silly-Nah is missing."

Nina, laying out the heavy white plates, did not answer. She suspected Aunty Lee would lose interest once the poor dead woman's identity was revealed. It would probably be in tomorrow morning's newspapers, which was why Aunty Lee was milking the mystery for all it was worth now. Again she thought it was probably because she was bored.

"Aunty, you should play mah-jongg," Nina said. "Or go on a cruise."

"She may have been on a cruise!" Aunty Lee agreed. "And fell overboard. But that doesn't mean it wasn't murder. We should take note of any of the women who registered for tonight's dinner and don't show up . . ."

Going by the previous week's wine dining event, Nina would not have been surprised if at least one of the guests did not return. This was no reflection on the food, which had been good. Selina had worried about how spicy the food was but Mark had not seemed to mind, and all their paying guests had enjoyed their dinner. It was only after dinner that things had got interesting, as Aunty Lee had put it. Laura Kwee, the friend whom Mark and Selina had brought in to help serve the wine, had drunk enough to be embarrassingly chatty. Nina had been rather uncomfortable. But at least Aunty Lee was looking forward to today's dinner with all the relish of a child getting ready for school after a long, dull vacation alone.

And why shouldn't she? Nina reflected, taking her feelings out on the flattened sticks of satay before putting them in the enormous fridge in the back storeroom to await their grilling. Aunty Lee had been very nice to Laura, even letting her leave her things in the storeroom of the café that night because she had clearly been in no shape to get them as well as herself home. Laura had not returned to collect her bag either. Nina would not be surprised if Laura Kwee did not show up that night.

"I'm going to keep the TV on during tonight's dinner," Aunty Lee said. "Doesn't matter what the show is. Sometimes they have those breaking news announcements."

"Sir Mark doesn't like that." Nina knew Mark planned the music that accompanied his wines as carefully as Aunty Lee planned the serving dishes that presented her food.

"It's still my shop," Aunty Lee said firmly. "Besides, if we don't pay attention to what's happening, who is going to?"

Selina Khaw-Lee, wife of Aunty Lee's stepson, Mark, had not heard anything about the unidentified body found on Sentosa and would not have admitted it if she had. As Selina said disparagingly to anyone who invited her to their online networking sites, exercise classes, or volunteer work, "I have a life, you know!" After all, Selina had already started preparing to be a model mother. She had decided on names for her future children long before she had decided whom their father would be. And it was precisely for the sake of these future offspring that she took so much interest in her husband's business and prospects. The Lees were old money. In a young nation like Singapore, old money was anything that had been in a family for more than twenty years. Their lifestyle was one that Selina, the daughter of two teachers comfortably anchored in the middle of Singapore's respectable middle class, had always aspired to—she saw herself living the life of a Tai-Tai, wearing designer clothes and going for manicures and overseas holidays. Unfortunately her husband was also living a Tai-Tai lifestyle. Mark Lee had grown up with that comfortable nonchalance toward money that a financially privileged childhood confers. It didn't seem to matter to him that all his father's money had been stolen by his second wife. But it mattered to Selina.

"I don't think you should let Laura Kwee have any wine tonight. She's obviously not used to it."

"It's a wine-tasting dinner," Mark Lee said mildly. Mark was generally mild, especially where his wife was concerned. "Besides, Laura is helping me with the serving, right?"

"She didn't say she isn't coming. I texted her a reminder to give her a chance to back out if she wanted to—it would be just like her to back out at the last moment—but she just said 'see you there.' Not a word of apology. After carrying on like a drunken alcoholic!"

"Laura already apologized, right?" Mark slowed down to join the queue of cars waiting to cross the Bukit Timah Canal. The younger Lees lived in a condominium across the canal from Binjai Park. It was not a great distance—if not for the trees, you could see Aunty Lee's Delights from their ninth-floor apartment—but given the large canal and two main roads that separated them, only the servants walked in between. "Laura's not used to wine, that's all. If she was any kind of alcoholic, a few glasses of wine wouldn't have had any kind of effect on her."

Mark seldom disagreed with his wife, but he knew Selina was only venting in advance because she was steeling herself to keep up her social persona for the rest of the evening. Selina worried so much about what people were thinking of her that she was always uncomfortable in public. Mark was looking forward to the evening as he waited for traffic to clear. He was a patient driver. Selina was not patient about anything.

"Why did you let that car cut in like that? He has no right! Did you see what he did? If you didn't stop he would have caused an accident!" No response from Mark. "Did you remember to bring over all the wine yesterday?"

"All except the Albarino. I thought at first Chianti for the satay but then last night I thought about it, and I think the 2009 La Cana that just came in would do better. And I can talk a bit about Spanish wine. We've been having so much French and Australian lately."

"You want to open it because it just came," Selina said

sourly. "Is it expensive? I told you not to waste expensive stuff on these people. Anyway, that old woman's food is going to drown out all your wine as usual. They won't notice what they are drinking."

Mark did not answer.

"There's no point wasting that," Selina said sharply. "You know Aunty Lee can't tell the difference anyway. You could just get her some old bottle from the supermarket and she wouldn't notice."

"She likes it that I bring her something special," Mark said. "We're partners in this, after all."

Selina snorted. "You can wrap up any old bottle. She won't be able to tell the difference. If you ordered that specially, you should be able to sell it for more. Don't waste it."

It would not be a waste, Mark thought. Selina thought that wrapping a bottle in brown paper or a coat of aluminum foil would be enough for Aunty Lee. But the wine would not be wasted because he was really doing it for himself, and he appreciated it.

"They shouldn't notice what they are drinking. They shouldn't notice what they are eating. They shouldn't even notice how good they feel. Then we'll have got the pairing right."

Perhaps Mark could be a food critic—or a poet—if this latest venture of his failed like all the previous ones, Selina thought. Not for the first time she wondered whether she could still make it as a derivatives trader or real estate agent. If she made her own fortune, she could forget about pushing her husband into succeeding. But she wanted Mark to stay with this, she reminded herself. The Lee fortune was there for the taking even if Mark did not make a profit. And this latest brainwave gave her a chance to keep an eye on Aunty Lee's Delights. Even if Aunty Lee claimed she only ran the café as a hobby, it was clearly raking in cash. And since it had been set up by the late M. L. Lee with money that should have been Mark's, clearly Mark should be benefiting from the profits as well.

Selina conveniently forgot Mark's sister, who seemed quite happy with how things were. Anyway, Mathilda had never shown much interest in what was happening in Singapore.

"I hope Laura pulls herself together today." Selina returned to her current peeve. "Even before she turned into a lush, she was getting all the glasses mixed up."

"Maybe she won't turn up." Mark turned into Binjai Park. The row of shophouses, which housed a pizzeria and several antiques shops as well as Aunty Lee's Delights, stood on a side street to their left, separated from the main estate road by a decorative grass verge with the usual trees, shrubbery, and a metal prayer bin. "How many people signed up for tonight, anyway?"

"Why do you say that?" Selina asked, ignoring his question. "Do you think Laura won't be here tonight? She's supposed to come and help with every session. That's why we gave her a discount. What did she tell you?"

"Nothing. I can set up everything myself, that's all I

meant." Mark concentrated on parking. He stopped the CD player to concentrate, and the system switched automatically to radio.

Even if it wasn't a murder case, so gruesome to think of all those people enjoying themselves in the holiday resort while there's someone lying dead on the beach, don't you think?

Maybe it's a publicity stunt by the resort. Next they'll announce there's a murder mystery competition—dead body washed up on Sentosa, did the ghosts of murdered dolphins do it?

"I hate those radio commentators, they're so stupid!" Selina said. "Mark, what are you waiting for?"

Mark kept the engine on. He wanted to hear what else they had to say. But there was nothing more.

Harry Sullivan had arrived early, as he always did. He liked being on time. "Singapore time"—which could run up to thirty minutes behind any set appointment—was one of the things he disliked most about Singapore, and so, while he expected local people to be late for appointments, he himself refused to be late. Harry had never been particular about punctuality before; but here in Singapore, he was an expat, an *ang moh* and a man to be noticed.

Back in Oz, he had been stepped on and pushed aside by the greedy, grabbing new immigrants invited in by a soft government, but over here the tables were turned. He was aware that people looked at Mr. Harry Sullivan differently here and the change in him had come naturally in response to that. Harry liked what he had become in Singapore. He was full of new project ideas, his conversation sparkled and impressed even himself, and he was a hit with local women, who loved being seen with a white man. It almost made up for the humid, equatorial heat.

This evening he was wearing a red batik shirt (considered formal wear in the tropics) unbuttoned over a white T-shirt and Bermuda-length cargo pants. It was the third wine dining he was attending. Not that he didn't prefer beer to wine, but he was expected to maintain certain standards here in Singapore and he tried to live up to those expectations. He guessed the old Caucasian couple coming slowly along the five-foot way peering into shop windows and squinting at shop numbers had signed on for the same event at Aunty Lee's Delights as he had. They looked like retirees who were traveling to see the world and had chosen Singapore as their first stop because of its clean, safe, English-speaking reputation. Both with fuzzy-ginger-turning-gray hair and in matching Merlion T-shirts, they also looked new to Singapore and Southeast Asia. Harry Sullivan, with six months' residence behind him, could afford to be generous to these newcomers.

"Hey there. Here for the wine-and-local-food do?"

Frank and Lucy Cunningham were glad to see him. They were early, as Lucy explained. They had expected to get lost but they had not. Lucy was doing most of the talking, and Harry guessed the dinner—perhaps their whole trip—had been her idea.

"How many people attend these things?" Frank Cunningham wanted to know.

"First time ten people showed up," Harry answered. "Second time only six. I have no idea how many people will be turning up tonight, but the food is good. It's definitely an experience you won't get anywhere else."

"Oh goody," Lucy Cunningham said. She peered in through the window, but though she could discern two women pottering around inside, no one came to the door. "Doesn't look like they're going to be ready for a while. We'll go look around first. We saw an antique shop."

Typical tourist types, Harry Sullivan thought.

"So who is coming tonight?" Mark asked again.

Selina thought that her earlier silence should have made clear that this was not something she wanted to discuss. For a moment she wondered whether Mark was deliberately trying to provoke her, but one glance at him made her dismiss the thought. He looked as blandly uninvolved as that stepmother of his . . . which was good because Selina didn't know who was going to turn up that night. Laura Kwee was in charge of taking down the names and collecting payment. In the run-up to the previous two dinners, she had called or texted Selina every time someone called with an inquiry. Selina had made it very clear that this had to stop—"If you're going to bother me with every detail, I might as well do it myself!"—and since then, there had been no word from Laura Kwee.

Selina felt a quiver of foreboding that she tried to suppress. Perhaps she had spoken more sharply to Laura than she need have. Maybe she'd offended her. But that woman could be so dense sometimes. The shiver she felt was not exactly in her gut—more in her bladder. She wondered if there was time for Mark to drive her up to Aunty Lee's house to use the toilet. Selina did not use public toilets, not even the one at the wine café that was maintained daily by contract cleaners, supervised by Nina. It was not just a matter of cleanliness but of privacy. Selina could not bear the thought of any stranger using the toilet after she did. No matter how carefully one cleaned up, there were bound to be some traces left—it seemed to her the grossest invasion of privacy. But as Selina decided to get back in the car, Mark finished securing the travel case holding his precious wine bottles onto its wheeled trolley and locked the vehicle.

"Mark, I have to use the ladies'."

"No problem. You've got lots of time."

"Mark!"

Mark continued toward the entrance of the wine café without waiting for her or offering her his arm, as he used to do during their courtship and the early days of their marriage. Absurdly perhaps, she was now angry with her husband for not waiting for her to answer the question she had been angry with him for asking.

"I don't know," Selina called after him. "I have no idea who's turning up tonight. I don't even know how many people are coming—or if anybody is!"

It was ridiculous that she tried so hard to help him, she thought, when he was so ungrateful. Well, not exactly ungrateful; Mark was programmed with a reflex that made him say thank you, even to people like waiters and servants whom Selina did not notice. But at the same time he was so blindly unaware of how much Selina did for him all the time and every day. One day she would drum it into him in a way that he would never forget. It would be so satisfying to see him taken aback. And one day soon she would hit him with the information that would make him realize exactly how well she knew him and he'd never take her for granted again. But for now she hugged her delicious secret to herself. Some people could not keep a secret to save their lives. Selina Lee knew and had benefited from that failing. She held her own information close to her, enjoying the potential power it gave her. Feeling better, she followed Mark.

The back door to Aunty Lee's Delights was held open for them by Aunty Lee herself.

"We don't know how many people are coming for dinner tonight," Selina told her. "Laura Kwee was supposed to handle it and she never got back to me, it's not my fault."

"Ah, Silly-Nah!" Aunty Lee said. "Good, you are here. Laura Kwee already gave us thumb drive with info last week for all the sessions. Eight people for dinner tonight, nobody paid yet—ha ha—except you and Mark no need to pay of course! Did you hear about the body they found on Sentosa? Don't you think that the poor girl must have been murdered?"

"Oh no!" Mark said, stopping abruptly.

"Mark? What's wrong?"

"Nothing—just . . . the wineglasses are all wrong. And the circles on paper haven't been numbered."

"Laura will do that." Selina snapped out of her reverie. "She'll be here any minute now. I'll just give her a call."

"I don't think she's coming," Mark said. "Can you just—"

"She said she would do it!" Selina snapped. She turned away from him. It was no use trying to get a connection inside the shop. Selina was sure Aunty Lee's equipment was jinxing her phone signals.

Her phone bleeped a message announcement just as she reached the door. She pulled it out (she would have to remember to switch it to "silent" later—Mark hated being interrupted). Once she saw whose phone it was from, Selina already guessed the message. "You two go ahead, I have to take this," she said to Mark and Aunty Lee. They had already gone on to discuss glasses and marker pens with Nina.

The message was from Laura Kwee's phone.

Sorry not feeling well, can't make it tonight. Marianne said she can't come either. It was signed with Laura's usual smiley face.

It looked as though Laura Kwee, dense or not, had taken offense after all. Selina's lips tightened. She did not have time to play Laura's stupid games.

2

Wine Dining

"So no Laura Kwee means no live entertainment tonight!" Aunty Lee chuckled when Selina passed the news to her.

"She said Marianne Peters isn't coming either," Selina said, not laughing.

"No, Marianne is out of Singapore," Cherril Lim-Peters said, entering just then. "And Mycroft isn't coming either, he sends his apologies."

"Oh. Why?" Selina was peeved. She had already told several people that Mycroft Peters was part of their dining club. He was a high-profile lawyer and NMP—nominated member of parliament—and Selina considered his wife a poor substitute. Cherril did not even speak good English.

"He had something on tonight."

"You reserved three places. This is going to upset our seating plans." The least the woman could do was offer to pay for her absent relatives. The Peters family was rich enough.

"So sorry. But something came up." Cherril handed Selina precisely seventy dollars for herself. Selina preferred not to deal money openly so they could all keep up the impression this was a social occasion, a gathering of friends. That was why Laura Kwee had been brought in to help. But Laura Kwee was not there and money was money. Selina took it.

"It's eighty dollars," Selina said stiffly.

"Mycroft said you told him seventy. I'm getting the ticket under his name."

Actually Cherril had left Mycroft Peters comfortably at home, dining with his parents.

Cherril Lim-Peters was under no illusions. She had been a flight attendant before her marriage and Selina Lee was not the only one to turn up her middle-class nose because of that. But Cherril was trying to learn social graces and this wine dining was a good opportunity. Cherril had learned a lot during the previous couple of weeks—and not just about food and wine. She had been eager to return even if her husband was not. Mycroft had said it was up to her.

The Peters family had long been friends of Aunty Lee and her late husband. They lived along Binjai Rise much farther into the same housing estate. Renovations had added a two-story wing with a kitchenette and an additional domestic helper to the household so that Cherril and Mycroft had some privacy, though the whole family still sat down to dinner together every night. Cherril, who had been used to eating in front of the television or computer when not swallowing instant noodles standing in the galley, had found these dinners difficult to get used to—but things were not as bad since Mycroft's sister, Marianne, had gone off on holiday. And without Mycroft or Marianne around, Cherril hoped to get something out of that evening's wine dining that would make things even better.

There were not going to be eight people at that evening's wine dining after all.

From his comfortable smoking spot behind the tall potted plants edging the sidewalk, Harry Sullivan watched the people gathering inside. Though he liked being punctual, he didn't like hanging around inside waiting for food to be served. It made him look too hungry and eager to please. He glanced at his reflection in the window of Aunty Lee's Delights. Though the lights were on inside, it was still bright enough outside for him to see himself clearly reflected. It was not a bad picture. His hair was still all his own and still close to the brown black of the photograph in his passport. Standing five foot eight, he had been considered short back home, but here he was comfortably average. And he guessed he was more than average in other departments too, going by the feedback he had received. He allowed himself a small smile at the memory.

Yes, Harry Sullivan was definitely looking forward to
tonight's dinner, even aside from the food that he could
see being prepared now. A dim shape waved at him from
the interior and he waved back, automatically assuming
the genial grin that these people expected of him. Did they
really think that all Aussies ate nothing but beef and drank
nothing but beer? He could so easily have found their attempts to introduce him to Asian food and European beer
bloody condescending. Even if he had chosen to stay away
from Chinese food and snob wines, there was nothing in
this pretentious little city he could not have found back
home . . . he reminded himself he was only leading them
on. He enjoyed this. He was the white sahib here. When he
was ready, when he had made his money and established
himself, he would lay it all out for them, of course. And
these people would finally know how much more he had
known than they did all along.

"Harry! I thought I saw you out here. I thought you were
always early—can't wait, huh?" Mrs. Selina Lee stuck out
her head, tilted girlishly. "Why don't you come on inside
and join the others? There'll be some of your countrymen
coming tonight." She laughed.

Harry could tell that she fancied him. She was flirting
with him with her husband right inside, no doubt dust-
ing fingerprints off his glasses with his fancy cloths. He
responded automatically. "I couldn't wait to see you!" he
said gallantly, flirting to order as he finished his cigarette
and stubbed it out in the pot of bamboo by the entrance.

Normally Selina would have told customers not to smoke there, right outside the café, because there was a law against it. But she liked Harry Sullivan and there was no reason to put him in a bad mood. Selina made a mental note to tell Nina to put up a "No Smoking" sign. Aunty Lee should have done that. After all, it was her food that was being affected.

"Have you seen the latest *Island High Life*? There's a review of the café in it. Here . . ." He handed her the magazine with a wink. "You may be running this place soon!"

"Ooh, you're terrible. You shouldn't say such things!" Selina said primly with delight. "Coming in? They're not ready, of course, but you can sit down and have a drink first." She lowered her voice conspiratorially. "We're all having a good gossip about the body on Sentosa. Aunty Lee loves mysteries. That's why everything is running late tonight."

"Last cigarette," Harry Sullivan told her. Just then Mark Lee appeared. He was wearing a blue-and-red paisley bow tie and a light blue suit, and Harry, who had an eye for these things, could tell at once that the man was a poof even if he didn't know it himself.

"Selina, have you seen my Montblanc?" Mark asked. "I just put it down for a moment and it's gone. Can you ask Nina if she's seen it?"

Ignoring her husband, Selina pouted at Harry Sullivan. "You really shouldn't smoke so much, you know. Well, come in when you're ready!"

As they moved into the shop and he pulled out his half-empty pack of menthols (cigarettes were bloody pricey here), he could hear the woman going, "Did you hear what Harry Sullivan said to me? He said he came early because he couldn't wait to see me!" It took so little, he thought, to keep a woman happy. It was a wonder more men didn't realize and take advantage of that fact.

He returned his lighter to his fanny pack. It was not exactly formal wear but useful for carrying things safely with no awkward bulges and was in keeping with his white-man-in-the-tropics image. Besides, he rather liked seeing Mark Lee wince. Mark Lee might think he had such high standards, but no matter what he dressed himself in, he was nothing more than an upstart Chink. It was definitely an advantage to be a single Caucasian man in Singapore, Harry thought. Even these wine-enhanced dinners were part of it.

When they first approached him, Selina Lee and Laura Kwee had made it clear that he was precisely the sort of patron (yes, Selina had said "patron," which made him feel he was supporting a college or a hospital rather than a dinner club) they were looking to attract and had given him a very generous discount to boot. He had checked, of course, automatically distrusting people who talked about special deals. And he had learned from others at that first dinner party that they had indeed paid a whopping eighty dollars per head—double what he had been charged. It had made him enjoy the proceedings all the more. And of course he had found their later confrontations highly enjoyable. There was nothing more entertaining than watching women lose their tempers and take it out on each other—especially when you knew that at some level it was you they were fighting over.

Even though it was almost seven, he could see they were still messing around with table arrangements.

"Laura Kwee was supposed to be here early, to help Mark set out the wineglasses. Now it seems she's decided not to show up," Selina explained to the room in general.

Even though the wine was being served in the company of food (a big no-no for any genuine tasting), Mark maintained the need for separate glasses. For tonight, that meant four glasses per person to be set up at their places and filled precisely to the widest point in each glass at least fifteen minutes before the wines were to be sampled. After the confusion of the first wine dining, Mark now insisted on numbered coasters being set at each place so it would be clear to everyone which wine he was discussing.

"Nina, don't keep messing with the plates. We can't start until the coasters are ready, so go and help Mark write down the numbers!"

"What numbers should I write, sir?"

"Don't worry, Nina. I'll take care of it. Go and take all the glasses off the table so that I can arrange them on the coasters once they're dry."

At least when Selina was head prefect in school, she had gotten some credit for her ability to maintain order. But now her efforts were just ignored, criticized, or taken for granted. She supposed this was how the PAP felt. Not for the first time Selina wondered about joining Singapore's omnipotent People's Action Party . . . after all, Mycroft Peters himself must have put his name forward. But she had more immediate things to deal with; and even if Mark and Aunty Lee resisted her best efforts to organize their lives, she would get the dinner in order somehow.

As Mark fiddled, Selina watched what she could see of Harry Sullivan through the window. He glanced at the bamboo pot, looked around, and finally dropped his cigarette butt in the metal prayer bin standing on the road nearby. It was not yet the Ghost Month, but people still used the bin—foreign laborers and maids, Selina suspected. Fruits, flowers (obviously stolen from National Parks bushes), and even joss sticks often appeared on makeshift altars around the bin.

At that moment the Cunninghams, even though they were already late, stopped to photograph the bin and the makeshift altar beside it. Selina bit back her irritation at the sight of them. As Mark was always reminding her, what other people did was not her business.

"Everything's very expensive here," Lucy Cunningham said, "but it's so clean and so efficient and everybody speaks English. It's already starting to feel like coming back home!" She was a comfortably plump woman who seemed content to look her age; no signs of cosmetic surgery or even hair coloring. But in spite of her chatter, Mrs.

Cunningham looked unhappy. This was not unusual for a woman her age. What was unusual was that her face did not look used to being unhappy. It kept lapsing into contentment and even curiosity and then, as if triggered by a thought or memory, it would cloud over again.

Aunty Lee wondered what was causing this. Because under her surface coating of worry, Lucy Cunningham emitted a glow of contentment. She also had the body of a happy woman, and at moments when she forgot her unhappiness, she took in everything around her with calm, unaffected interest. Perhaps she was suffering from food poisoning, Aunty Lee thought, or an argument with the husband.

"It's so good of you to include us at such short notice. And I'm sorry we were late, but we took a walk and there was this antique shop and Frank saw some wood carvings he wanted to take a closer look at. He's very interested in wood."

Mrs. Cunningham had not argued with her husband, Aunty Lee decided.

Selina was gracious as she collected money from the Cunninghams.

"So glad we're getting a chance to experience typical Singapore dining!"

Selina hoped the Cunninghams didn't think they were in for a "typical Singapore" experience. The whole point of what they were trying to do was to lift their wine café experience to a level above what was "typical" for Singapore.

Well, that was where Aunty Lee's cooking would come in use, she supposed. No one could say *nonya* cuisine was not typically Singaporean. But still, Selina thought wistfully of the day when she could get Mark a place of his own. They would have more class than this café. She would serve bread sticks, perhaps cheese and grapes like she had seen in an Island City brochure . . . when she looked up from her daydream, Aunty Lee had gone—

Selina found Nina, who was flaming sticks of satay over the charcoal brazier in the alley just outside the back door of the shop.

"Do you know did Aunty Lee see this month's *Island High Life* magazine yet?"

Nina looked blankly at her. "Sorry, ma'am?"

Sometimes Selina wondered whether Nina was deliberately acting stupid. No one could be as slow as she was. When Selina did not answer immediately, Nina turned back to the row of satay sticks she was squatting over.

Nina had put on weight since she started working for Aunty Lee, Selina thought. When she first saw her, Nina had been a scared, skinny little thing who had cried when she could not understand what Mark meant when he insisted on her finding their "special cups"—the glass cups that were kept just for Mark and Selina because they could not drink out of the unbreakable plastic cups Aunty Lee had bought for use in the house. Aunty Lee had even fed Nina the Brands Essence of Chicken that people had given her for Chinese New Year. "Too rich for me," the old woman said. "The girl needs more strength, more meat on her bones!" Selina had been so furious. Whoever heard of feeding Brands to maids? And those were new bottles, not even expired stock that would otherwise be discarded. Selina was married to the son of the house and Aunty Lee had never worried about her health or offered her Brands Essence.

Selina had been sore enough to refuse to let Mark visit Aunty Lee for two weeks, pointedly saying they were too busy with work and too tired from doing business research and market studies (not surprising since no one thought to offer them the expensive supplements that were lavished on servants). This tactic had always worked with her own parents, but sadly Aunty Lee accepted their absence so stoically that Selina had caved first.

It was not the first time Nina had made life hard for Selina. When she first arrived in the household, Selina had even warned Aunty Lee that having a young servant in the house with an old man like M. L. Lee was dangerous. "Men are all the same. They get taken in by a pretty face, they feel sorry for her. Next thing you know, she's got her claws into him!" But though Aunty Lee had thanked her and promised to keep an eye on Nina, she had not done anything as far as Selina could see. In fact she had bought Nina new clothes ("Because people work better in the right clothes") and sent her for driving lessons and computer classes ("Because two old people like us, we need someone young with good eyes to keep us in touch with the world!"). Nina was still far from fat but she was no longer skinny. And in her loose brown slacks and long cream tunic top, she did not fit Selina's idea of how a foreign domestic worker should dress.

"Are you pregnant?" Selina asked sharply. It would be typical of Aunty Lee to allow Nina to go out without supervision. Selina was well versed in the maid horror stories that revolved around lovers, stolen food and jewelry, and prostitution.

"Sorry, ma'am?" Still looking blank, Nina started to remove the satay onto a waiting plate, already lined with a trimmed banana leaf.

"I'm talking to you—please stop that and pay attention to me!"

"Is something the matter?" Aunty Lee popped up in the doorway. "Nina, watch the satay, ah, don't let it get burned, otherwise we are all going to be in big trouble!"

Nina turned back to the satay and left her boss to handle Selina.

"I was just asking Nina—whether you had seen the latest *Island High Life* magazine," Selina said. "I didn't want to ask you in case you hadn't seen it and got upset." Even to Selina, this didn't sound quite right. "Because I didn't want you to be upset, I mean. So I wanted to warn her to be sure to keep it away from you."

"What magazine?" asked Aunty Lee. "I don't read magazines. Nina, did you remember to add the tamarind juice to the peanut sauce or not?"

"Yes, ma'am. Added already."

"I didn't want you to be upset," Selina said almost desperately, "because it had a review of the café in it and it didn't say very nice things."

"Did it? Luckily I don't read such things. Finished, Nina? Be careful. Don't drop anything. Carry in and put on the table. Make sure you don't move any of Mark's precious glasses!"

Back inside, Frank Cunningham was fooling around with the paper napkins. Mark and his precious glasses were almost ready, Selina saw with some relief. She didn't know anything about wine and frequently confused the bottles when she was trying to help her husband.

"This," said Frank with boyish pride, "is for you." He held up a paper napkin folded into a miniature replica of the Sydney Opera House and handed it to Cherril Lim-Peters. Cherril squealed with delight. Selina turned away to get more paper napkins—she would keep Frank Cunningham's replacement napkin aside so as not to encourage the man, but she wanted to have it on hand so that when the dinner (finally) started, she could hand it to him with a reproving look.

"Can you believe it? It's so incredible!" Cherril took out her cell phone to take a photograph of the paper replica. "I have to send this to Mycroft!"

Selina didn't like Cherril—she was a stewardess and Selina could tell from her spoken English (fluent but flawed) that she was not of their class and brought down the tone of their gatherings. But as always, Mark pretended not to understand.

"We don't have any class," he had said. "My great-grandfather made money by putting rubber tires on rick-shaws. Anyway, Cherril knows more about wine than most of the other people who come." Mark and Cherril had met at a wine tasting, and thanks to her travels and interest, she sometimes came across interesting wine producers and dealers whom she put Mark in touch with. That was the other and main reason Selina disliked her.

"We're from Sydney," Lucy Cunningham was saying in her gentle, cultured voice. "Frank likes to make that wher-ever we go—just for a while there's a little bit of Sydney here."

"Oh, Harry is from Sydney too." Selina recalled herself to her duties as hostess. "Have you been introduced? Frank and Lucy Cunningham, this is Harry Sullivan."

"Sydney's a big, big place," Harry said.

"Harry Sullivan . . ." Frank said thoughtfully. "I know the name and you even look familiar . . . you're much too young to know old geezers like us—are you named after your old man? An uncle maybe?"

"No. Sydney's a big place, Sullivan's a common name," Harry said. "So what brings you guys to Singapore?"

It was a question any tourist might expect to be asked, often without any interest whatsoever on the part of the asker. Anything along the lines of "seeing the world now we're retired" would probably have done the trick. But

Lucy looked guiltily at her husband, who ducked his head and said, "Nothing. Nothing."

"Have you two been here before?" Immediately Aunty Lee's rat-scenting antenna was waving wildly.

"No, no. We've never been in this part of the world before. And it's just chance, pure chance, that we decided to take a look in here for dinner tonight."

Mark Lee crushed the napkin he was holding into a crumpled ball and put it on the table next to the Sydney landmark. "That's the Esplanade," he said. "Our national landmark." He laughed. Others laughed too. Later, thinking about the six-hundred-million-dollar spiked domes that graced (or disgraced) the Singapore waterfront, Selina thought it very witty of Mark. But at the time she was anxious to get started and irritated by the waste of another napkin. She was also irritated by how clever Cherril Lim-Peters seemed to find the remark.

"Can we all sit down and get started? We're late already."

In the manner common to such occasions, hungry guests did not want to seem to be in a hurry to eat (convention did not allow you to say you were starving till seated) and harried hosts could not rush guests through cocktails and conversation no matter how worried they were about dishes overcooking or rapidly cooling.

Mark, who was normally more focused where his precious wine was concerned, was deep in conversation with Cherril Lim-Peters, who was saying something about "suppliers I met while traveling in the Loire Valley," and Selina cut her off with a chilly smile. "Excuse me. We're running late as it is."

"I've got the names of some reliable suppliers," Mark said to Cherril. "But if we really want to make it work, we should plan a face-to-face meeting. I find those are always more productive."

"I only have a week there while Mycroft is having meetings in Paris . . ." Cherril simpered. "Unless I make a special trip."

"Mark, please. I have to talk to you now!"

Selina clamped a hand just above Mark's elbow and dragged him away physically. Selina didn't like Cherril Lim, though not in the same way she disliked Laura Kwee, Marianne Peters, Nina, or Aunty Lee. There were so many reasons to dislike women, just as there were so many reasons to despise men.

When they finally sat down to the table, it was almost twenty minutes after the stated time, but no one seemed surprised. Selina insisted on the television and radio being turned off.

"But I want to know if they find out who the woman on Sentosa is!"

Aunty Lee seemed determined to talk about the body, as though by discussion she could ferret out more information than she had gotten off the radio and the afternoon paper. Selina ignored her.

The Cunninghams seemed more interested in learning

about Sentosa than about the dead woman found on one of its beaches.

"We heard about the casino, of course. I thought it might be fun. But Frank wants to go take photographs at Universal Studios."

"There are wild peacocks there," Cherril Lim-Peters said vaguely. "I like peacocks."

Prodded by Selina, Mark rose to his feet at his place at the head of the table. He reached over and picked up the silver slosh bucket closest to him. "Just to follow protocol," he announced. "You won't need these with my wines, but I must ask you not to use them for the food!" It was the same way he had introduced the previous wine-dine. People had laughed then and he was not about to change anything that worked.

Cherril giggled prettily. Then, thinking Selina looked puzzled, she started to explain to her what a slosh bucket was for . . .

"First course!" Aunty Lee announced as Nina entered from the back, bearing two platters of hot satay flanked by thinly sliced cucumbers and tomatoes and cubes of rice cake fragrantly steaming with the scent of *pandan*.

Mark took them through a white, a rosé, and three red dinner wines before dessert. Only Cherril was paying rapt attention and asking the occasional question, but it was enough for Mark . . . and enough for Selina too, who resolved to keep an eye on the woman. From Selina's point of view, no one could be that interested in wine—therefore Cherril had to be interested in Mark. That Cherril already had a husband of her own made no difference to Selina except as evidence that Cherril knew how to trap men. Aunty Lee was watching Cherril too—ever since she saw the girl rinse out her mouth with water between mouthfuls of food as well as between mouthfuls of wine.

"Why you rinse and spit? That is not wine, what?" Aunty Lee asked. "You don't like my gravy, is it?"

"Oh no! It's very good!" Cherril said earnestly. "But this way I can start with a clean mouth for the next mouthful and I don't confuse the taste. Your gravy is very good, Aunty Lee. Everything is very good. But I want to enjoy it as though every mouthful is the first mouthful!"

"Keep the bloom, eh?" Harry Sullivan said. "It's like they say about marriage. The first three years are great, but you have to pay for them for the rest of your life!" He laughed loudly. "That's why some guys keep getting married. Just keep going through those first three years over and over again!"

Perhaps this comment was directed at the married couples present? Selina wondered, watching Mark covertly. If he laughed, she would remember to be angry with him later. Selina did not like male-chauvinistic jokes and resented Mark for not putting them down more actively. Lucy Cunningham, meanwhile, smiled at her husband, who had joined in the laughter.

"That's what I say too," Frank said with gusto. "Keep

starting over. We all should remember to keep starting over. Every day, every season. That's the great thing about being able to travel like we do. We keep starting over. And we get to start over with the people we like best!" He had been playing around with his second napkin and had now produced a paper rose with a long twisted stem, which he presented to his wife with a flourish.

Cherril squeaked and applauded. "So romantic, you two!"

What an act, Selina thought. She was irritated with Cherril for all her fluttering as well as with the Cunninghams. Who did they think they were fooling? Traveling together was never easy, especially not with someone you had been married to for years, whose every word, said and unsaid, irritated you . . . and why wasn't Mark keeping better order?

Aunty Lee watched everyone at the table with interest. "Nice to see married people still being romantic," she said vaguely. "After so many years, you know what each other like, don't like already. Can be very good or can be very bad."

Nina, carrying in a tray of little orange-and-white ceramic bowls (Aunty Lee liked her food to look good) of *bubor cha cha*, thought that had certainly been the case with Aunty Lee and her husband. It had been very good while he was alive, no doubt. But once he was gone, wasn't it worse than losing a husband you had not cared about? She saw Harry Sullivan lean over to whisper something to Selina, who laughed. They shared a common sense of humor, Nina thought. She was careful around Selina, not wanting to upset someone who was so easily upset. But she was not afraid of her. Aunty Lee had made it clear that Nina's job depended on Aunty Lee alone, not any tales that anyone else might carry back to her.

"And now, as we prepare for the dessert, let me ask you to pick up glass number five." Mark had drawn and numbered circles on the strips of white paper set at each place. Even without Laura Kwee or anyone else to assist him, he had managed to set things up remarkably fast. "Most people assume dessert wines are sweeter wines. No doubt if you're planning to have nothing but wine for dessert, that would suit very well. But in my opinion, when we have a very sweet dessert as we are having tonight—*bubor cha cha*, right, Aunty Lee?—I believe a slightly fortified wine would accompany it better. See what you think of this. It's a discovery of mine I'm quite pleased with. You'll see it has something almost approaching the aura of an amontillado sherry . . ."

All at the table dutifully sipped as Aunty Lee found it necessary to interject in a loud whisper, "My *bubor cha cha* is not too sweet. Some people like to make it very sweet, but my one I make it not so sweet. You must have the contrast between the sweet potatoes and yam and the sweet soup . . ."

"Aunty Lee, we're not here to talk about the food," Selina said with an apologetic smile around the table as Frank Cunningham asked:

"What exactly goes into *bubor cha cha*?"

This was precisely the scenario Selina had been most dreading. The wine and Mark's exposition were forgotten as Aunty Lee went into how important it was that the tapioca jelly should be properly chewy and starchy and how she deliberately used sweet potatoes in different colors—purple, orange, and yellow—as well as yam, not only for the way the dish looked but because when the coconut milk was not too sweet, a discerning eater could tell the differences among them by both taste and texture. "And of course I use my special secret ingredient for the coconut milk soup . . ."

The bell over the front door of the shop jangled just then. Selina rose to her feet even as Nina stopped distributing bowls and started over to look. They were all congregated in the long back portion of the shop, but the lights were still on and Nina thought someone had come in looking perhaps for a bottle of *achar* or a late-night snack. Selina was certain it was Laura Kwee, finally showing up with some stupid excuse for her lateness.

As it turned out, they were both wrong.

It was difficult to tell the ethnic makeup of the woman who suddenly pushed through the front entrance of the shop. From her body language Nina thought her probably American—but there was a distinctly Oriental cast to her features. Her hair was very black—far more black than any naturally black hair could be—and her skin was pale beneath the reddish spottiness that Caucasian flesh tended to develop after recent and unfamiliar exposure to the Singapore sun and damp.

"Sorry. We're closed," Selina said firmly. She could tell at a glance that this intruder was no potential customer. Most likely she was lost and wanting directions, free water, or worse—use of the toilet.

The woman did not pay any attention to her.

"I'm looking for Laura Kwee," she said. "I heard she works here and I was told she would be here tonight." Dismissing Selina after a quick examination, the woman looked around her toward the people sitting at the table in the back room. "I have to talk to her. It's really urgent. Where's Laura Kwee?"

It was obviously urgent to her. It also seemed obvious she was not familiar with the Laura Kwee she was looking for. She was tense, almost trembling with anxiety barely kept under control. She hardly glanced at Aunty Lee as the old woman approached, eyes gleaming with interest.

"Who are you?" Aunty Lee asked. "Why are you looking for Laura Kwee? Laura doesn't work here. She is supposed to come tonight but she's not here yet. Why don't you come in and sit down to wait?"

"Laura Kwee's not coming tonight," Selina said firmly. The whole point of insisting that people register for the wine-and-dine special nights would be lost if the old woman was going to let in anybody who just decided to drop in. "She messaged me saying she can't make it. And she said Marianne Peters asked her to say she's not coming either."

The stranger seemed to gasp for air. She stared at Selina with fierce intensity and repeated, "Marianne Peters said she's not coming? When? When did she say that?"

"Who are you?" Aunty Lee asked. Suddenly she was by the woman's side, exuding the calm authority animal handlers display when dealing with nervous, possibly dangerous dogs. "I'm Aunty Lee. This is my shop. What's your name?"

"Carla Saito," the stranger replied.

In the silence that followed this announcement, Nina heard Lucy Cunningham whisper to her husband, "Why did Laura Kwee ask us to meet her here tonight if she's not coming?"

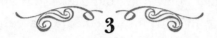

3

Where Is Laura Kwee?

"Come and sit down," Aunty Lee invited Carla Saito. Without seeming to have moved, Nina had a place setting ready and crowned with a bowl of *bubor cha cha*. Aunty Lee steered the tall, thin woman toward it with a firm grip just above her elbow and got her seated.

"Carla Saito . . . Is your name Japanese? Where are you from? Why are you looking for Laura Kwee? Do you know Marianne Peters too?"

Carla Saito looked at the bowl in front of her. "What is it? I don't eat meat."

In response to a nod from Aunty Lee that no one else noticed, Nina brought a little pot of (calming and restorative) chrysanthemum tea that she now put with a matching cup in front of the unexpected guest. "No meat," Aunty Lee said. The hot tea seemed to help and Carla Saito started to answer Aunty Lee's questions. She was American (her surname came from her Japanese father) and she had arranged to meet up with her old friend Marianne Peters in Singapore—only Marianne seemed to have disappeared.

"I was just going to wait. I mean, I came in a few days earlier than planned, so I thought maybe she was busy or out of the country or something. I thought I would just wait. She has to surface sooner or later, right? But then Marianne just didn't show up. I tried to ask her family but they said she's away, out of the country. Then just this afternoon I heard about a woman's body that was found—"

Aunty Lee nodded vigorously. "I also heard! A woman's dead body found on Sentosa!"

"And I suppose I just panicked. I started imagining all kinds of horrible things—I know it sounds ridiculous but if—"

"Why did you come here to look for her?" Aunty Lee asked. Her face was kind and concerned, her complexion so beautifully fine that even the papery wrinkles that appeared as she smiled spoke of gentle affection rather than age. But then Aunty Lee sniffed and looked puzzled. She looked at Carla Saito, who was sipping from her glass of chrysanthemum tea, then leaned in slightly closer and sniffed again. For a moment Aunty Lee looked more like a sniffer dog than a human cook.

"What is it?" Carla Saito asked.

Aunty Lee looked delighted to be asked. "You smell healthy," she said.

Carla Saito shook her head. "I'm far from healthy. It's not just jet lag. I've been so stressed, I haven't been sleeping. Even if I could I swear there are bedbugs in the sheets and—"

"You have healthy blood," Aunty Lee interrupted. "Just now you said you don't eat meat. Are you vegetarian?"

Carla Saito was surprised out of her problems. "Yes— well, actually I'm a vegan. But since coming here, I don't know—food isn't always labeled, at least not in English, and I can't figure out how to explain to people, so I've been eating mostly apples and bananas—"

"You just have to go near the temples to eat," Aunty Lee told her. "Near temples, sure to have hawker center or food court with vegetarian food. Do you eat onion and garlic?"

"Onion? Yes, sure . . ." Carla Saito glanced quickly round the room. No one else seemed surprised by this. Selina was rolling her eyes after giving up on trying to get Nina to stop Aunty Lee. Harry Sullivan was listening with detached interest—and helping himself to more wine. Carla could have used some of that wine or ideally something even stronger, but she went on sipping her tea. It was warming her faster than she thought possible and she realized how cold she had been. She hadn't been eating enough, of course, and her blood sugar and circulation were probably down.

"I put some ginger in," Aunty Lee said, sounding as

proud of herself as if she had been actually mind reading. "That should warm you up. Then, after that, you can eat some vegetarian food."

"It's not just vegetables, you know," Carla Saito said, wavering between caution and suspicion. "Just because you take the chicken or the pork or whatever out of the pot, it doesn't mean the vegetables inside are vegetarian."

Surprisingly it was Lucy Cunningham who spoke up. "Some traditional Buddhists are vegetarian on the first and fifteenth day of the lunar month. And most eat vegetarian on the first day of the lunar new year, which was last week. That's why you can probably get a wider range of vegetarian food than you get in Europe, for example."

"Right! Right! True! True!" Aunty Lee said, as though praising a smart student.

"Lucy reads up on stuff like that and tells me," Frank said. He looked pleased. "Some of it actually sticks, believe it or not." His wife gave a polite smile but seemed preoccupied. There was definitely something bothering her, Aunty Lee thought, and normally she would have probed further. But at the moment she had more fascinating fish to fry.

"You do look familiar," Frank continued to Harry Sullivan. "Any relatives we might know?"

"No brothers, no cousins. Sorry, mate."

"Trace far back enough, we all have common ancestors," said Frank Cunningham. "Whether it's the apes or Adam, eh?"

"As long as we keep reproducing, we'll all be related!" Harry Sullivan said. "Of course there's no guarantee of that. Not with all these left-wing gay activists running around saying men should marry men and women should marry women and babies can be aborted, no questions asked—"

Harry was looking at Carla Saito as he spoke, but it was Frank Cunningham who responded.

"Reminds me of a story I know—"

Lucy Cunningham shook her head but did not even try to stop her husband.

"An old cowboy sat down at the bar and ordered a drink. As he sat sipping his drink, a young woman sat down next to him. She turned to the cowboy and asked, 'Are you a real cowboy?'

"He replied, 'Well, I've spent my whole life breaking colts, working cows, going to rodeos, fixing fences, pulling calves, bailing hay, doctoring calves, cleaning my barn, fixing flats, working on tractors, and feeding my dogs, so I guess I am a cowboy.'

"She said, 'I'm a lesbian. I spend my whole day thinking about women. As soon as I get up in the morning, I think about women. When I shower, I think about women. When I watch TV, I think about women. I even think about women when I eat. It seems that everything makes me think of women.'

"A little while later, a man sat down on the other side of the old cowboy and asked, 'Are you a real cowboy?'

"He replied, 'I always thought I was, but I just found out I'm a lesbian.'"

Frank Cunningham roared with laughter as he delivered his punch line. Following his cue, Mark Lee and Harry Sullivan laughed too. Selina Lee and Lucy Cunningham appeared not to have heard anything, and Cherril Lim-Peters said:

"I don't understand. How can a man be a lesbian?"

Aunty Lee knew it would be no use trying to get Carla Saito to say more—at least not before she got some nourishment inside her. Aunty Lee could tell the girl had not eaten for some time—her body was exhausted and on guard.

Nina brought out a tureen of hot and sour soup (defrosted in the microwave, as it was an emergency) that she placed in front of Aunty Lee.

"You try this. You will like it. Then you can tell us all about why you are looking for Laura Kwee and why you are running around Singapore in the middle of the night without eating properly." Aunty Lee ladled out a generous bowlful of the soup and pushed it in front of Carla Saito expectantly.

"What's in it?" Carla knew she would probably eat it no matter what the answer was—now that she was sitting down, with the worst of her immediate fears allayed, she realized how hungry she was.

"Mushroom stock. My own homemade mushroom

stock. I use shiitake and wood ear both. Then got bamboo shoots, water chestnuts, and fried tofu. You said you can eat onion and garlic, right? For seasoning, there's onion and garlic and my homemade vinegar and homemade chili oil as well as pepper and hot sauce. Is it too hot? If too hot, you should take some rice . . . Nina?"

Nina was already on hand with the rice.

"And, Selina, why don't you try phoning Laura Kwee again."

"Aunty Lee, I told you Laura already said she won't be coming tonight."

"She doesn't have to come. I just want to talk to her."

Selina tried Laura's cell phone again. Again there was no answer.

Mark and Cherril were the only ones still at the table in the inner room discussing wine. Or rather, Mark was talking about wine and Cherril was listening, all agog, prompting him with questions. Nina had already started clearing the table, though Selina had not yet touched her dessert. Selina would have to speak to Aunty Lee about training the girl better. She avoided Aunty Lee's desserts as a matter of course, not just because she was worried about her weight but because all that coconut milk was seriously unhealthy. But it was still only right that Nina should have asked her before removing her untouched bowl. The Cunninghams, carrying their bowls with them, were walking around the shop looking at the paintings and jars of food on display.

Harry Sullivan, having abandoned his dessert but taking his wineglass and a bottle with him, had positioned himself at the table beside Aunty Lee and the strange woman.

"No need to panic," Harry said. "Bodies are found in the ocean all the time. Just because your friend doesn't answer her phone doesn't mean she's dead! Look, here's Selina. Selina, you just heard from Laura, didn't you? And she said she just heard from Marianne? Selina, tell this worried young lady that Marianne's fine."

Selina nodded. "Yes. Not more than an hour ago. I don't know where your friend is, but she's fine."

Still, she took her phone outside to try again. She had a few choice words for Laura Kwee herself.

Laura did not answer her cell phone. At some level Selina had expected this. She was angry with herself for not having foreseen it. But then Selina always expected the worst of people. Her giving Laura a chance to redeem herself had been part of her attempt to show people—show Mark, really—that she could put things behind her and move on. Mark insisted on seeing her as unforgiving, said that she held on to grudges. Of course Selina had argued him down and made him take it back, but the words still stung. She kept coming across examples that proved how wrong he had been to judge her, and it frustrated her that Mark just held up his hands in mock surrender and said he had apologized, the case was closed. It was not just about saying sorry and forgetting it, Selina thought resentfully. Mark had not understood why he was wrong. He had just grown tired of talking to her and wanted to drop the subject.

"Anything wrong?" Harry Sullivan appeared on the five-foot way. Selina wondered whether he was already leaving and tried to remember whether he had paid for his evening.

"No—Laura Kwee's still not answering. I just left a message for her to call me back."

"Not likely she'll call back if she's not answering, is it?"

"At least when they ask me again where she is, I can say I've tried again."

Harry lit a cigarette before continuing. "The whole wine-tasting business is like a ritual, isn't it? Like the Japanese tea ceremony? It's very interesting to see how Mark manages to marry it with the serving of food. Can't be easy."

"It's not." Selina felt slightly placated.

"And your friend Laura, well . . ."

"Yes?"

"Laura isn't very used to drinking, is she?"

His wickedly conspiratorial whisper made Selina laugh. She instantly felt better. Most of Selina's life was spent suspecting and trying to sniff out conspiracies rather than being included in them. Of course, Harry Sullivan was right. Laura Kwee had been very silly at the last dinner and was probably still embarrassed. The only person this reflected badly on was Laura herself, not the organizers of the gathering, as any reasonable guest could see. Selina also liked the way Harry made her feel. They were not exactly flirting—Selina would never do anything like that—but she felt part of a larger, cosmopolitan world when she was around him.

"I hope you didn't mind the things Laura said to you last week," Selina said. "She didn't mean anything by them."

"Oh, I think she did," Harry said unexpectedly. "That's why they only came out of her when she was drunk. All the rest of the time it's repressed inside her. Probably good for her to let it all out once in a while. And today she was probably just too embarrassed to turn up."

That was true. It was such a mature way of looking at what had happened that Selina decided to adopt it herself. But she would still make sure that Laura Kwee knew how angry she was. No one would have cared if Laura decided not to show up, but she had phoned saying she would be there, indeed that she would be there early in order to help . . . For the first time a quiver of worry crossed Selina's mind. It was not like Laura at all not to show up. Laura liked to be in on things, carrying stuff and arranging stuff so that she could make people think she was active and busy and needed. It just wasn't like her not to turn up for an event like this evening's.

But as Harry Sullivan had just pointed out, Laura was probably embarrassed. She had really behaved very badly at the previous gathering, especially to him. "Oh, were we supposed to wait for you to talk about it? But I've already finished all my wine!" Laura Kwee had said to general laughter at the first dinner when Mark tried to draw their attention to the slightly sharper, woodier-tasting wine he had chosen in order to complement the richness of the *laksa* gravy.

Mark had only shaken his head slightly at Laura's words. To him, she was an idiot, but he knew that she meant well. The best thing to do in such circumstances was to just let things go. Arguing with idiots just made you look like an idiot too. But Laura had apologized so tearfully and profusely afterward that Mark and even Selina had been placated.

It was pleasant outside, away from the talk and all the activity that went on around a meal, Selina thought. Even the ashy nicotine odor of Harry's cigarette did not annoy her as much as it usually did.

"We should see what's happening inside," Harry said.

Inside, the conversation of most of the guests had shifted from the lesson in wine appreciation that had been planned, with only Mark and Cherril continuing talking softly about the wine business at the other end of the table.

Carla Saito found she was explaining things to herself as much as to these strangers . . . these kind strangers. The soup was delicious. Her body, contentedly digesting quality nourishment for the first time in a week and a half, finally relaxed.

"I came to Singapore to meet my friend Marianne Peters," she said. There were some nods of recognition.

"Can't be a close friend if she didn't tell you she was going to be out of Singapore!" Harry Sullivan said.

Carla did not dignify that with an answer. "I thought maybe something came up. I was just going to wait. She knew where I was going to be staying, so I thought if I just waited, she would get in touch. But then this morning, when I was in the taxi, the radio was on—"

Aunty Lee thumped her palm on the table in delight. "You heard about the body, right? I also heard about the body!"

Aunty Lee was only too happy. "They say that she is unidentified, so anybody who knows anything please get in touch. We should phone them and say that Laura Kwee is missing—Laura Kwee and Marianne Peters, both missing."

"No, they're not missing!" Selina snapped. "Aunty Lee, you're just being dramatic for nothing. I told you Laura Kwee texted me. She said she couldn't come. She didn't say she was being thrown into the sea or anything. And she said that Marianne told her she wasn't coming either. So please stop talking rubbish and wasting all our time! If you're so worried, why don't you call the police? Come on, Mark. Are you finished? We should start clearing up."

"I did call the police," Carla Saito said in a small voice. "But they couldn't tell me anything. I thought maybe if I could just find out something about the body they found . . . at least I could set my fears to rest." She looked at Selina, who was checking the bag of leftovers Nina had just handed her. "Do you know what time Marianne phoned Laura Kwee to say she wasn't coming?"

"Must have been sometime today," Selina answered. "Anyway, nice meeting you. Good-bye."

"I should be going too." Harry Sullivan stood and gave an enormous stretch. "Give me a ride out to the main road?" No one took the hint.

"Marianne came for the first wine dining session," Aunty Lee said. "She signed up for all five of them, right, Selina? She and her brother, Mycroft, and his wife, Cherril. But then only Cherril is still coming. The others didn't want to come back after that first time."

"They're busy," Cherril said quickly. "I mean Mycroft is busy. Something came up. You know what Mycroft is like. He never stops."

"Did Marianne know when you were coming to Singapore?" Aunty Lee asked Carla. "She's away, right, Cherril?"

"She went on some kind of diving holiday with friends. I think she said they where going somewhere in Sabah . . . Seaventures at Sipadan or something like that. But the phone signal isn't very good and there're no phone chargers there, so she's not taking calls. She said she'll let us know when she's coming back."

"Surely she must have said how long she's gone for."

"A lot of people took extra leave because of the Chinese New Year, so she may not be coming back until after the weekend," Selina pointed out.

"Aren't her parents worried they haven't heard from her?" Aunty Lee asked Cherril.

"They're always worried about everything," Cherril said. "In fact Dad Peters wanted to try to get in touch with her friends if she wouldn't take their calls. But Mycroft wouldn't let them fuss. He says the more they try to control Marianne, the more she will fight them, so they should just leave her to do her own thing and if she's in trouble she'll call."

"Why are you looking for Laura Kwee?" Aunty Lee asked Carla.

"She was helping Marianne. Or rather she was getting a friend of hers to help," Carla replied. "It's really this guy I'm hoping to get in touch with."

Cherril, happily high on her evening out without her husband, was getting ready to say her farewells. She looked around for Mark, but apparently he had already forgotten her. He was watching his stepmother. Mark knew from long experience that when Aunty Lee served someone with what he thought of as her "special food face" on, it meant she wanted something from them. It was thanks to that food face (and lamb kebabs specially marinated in paprika, coriander, and cardamom) that Mark had told Aunty Lee and his father about the money problems he and Selina were then facing . . . in spite of all his promises to Selina. Even though things had all worked out wonderfully, thanks largely to Aunty Lee, he suspected Selina had never forgotten the episode and never forgiven Aunty Lee for making him break his promise. Now Mark was just glad he was not the one facing the hot bowl of soup.

Besides, he was curious too. Either Aunty Lee's "kaypohness" was infectious or he just wanted to find out why someone would go to such lengths to track down Laura Kwee.

Cherril left and the Cunninghams asked for a taxi to take them back to their hotel—surprising Selina, who had not seen them as people who could afford to stay at the Raffles. She felt a pang that she had missed recognizing the Cunninghams for what they were. That was the problem with Australians playing tourist. They dressed for comfort and it was impossible to tell how much they were worth. Apart from Harry Sullivan, of course. At least Harry respected his hosts enough to dress decently when he came to the wine and dines.

Selina could see that Harry was also studying Carla Saito thoughtfully. She wondered if he had reached the same conclusion as she had. Surely it was obvious (to everyone except Aunty Lee) what kind of relationship this woman was having with Marianne Peters. Selina felt a throb of glee. It was not only her duty to warn Aunty Lee that this might not be the sort of person she wanted to encourage as a customer; it was also clearly Selina's duty to warn Mycroft Peters what kind of company his little sister had been keeping in America, and whom she had been making plans with. Selina had always felt that Mycroft Peters looked down on Mark and herself in spite of his stewardess wife. Well, she thought, at least Mark didn't have a perverted sister!

Meanwhile Nina had finished clearing up the table and washing up the kitchen and setting the *kueh* mixes for the following day in the enormous fridge . . . and still Aunty Lee was asking questions and Carla Saito was not answering them.

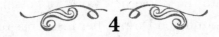

4

Laura Kwee on the Beach

News that a woman's (still-unidentified) body had been found on Sentosa was on the front page of the *Straits Times* the next morning. Nina could not see that there was anything more there than they had heard over the radio the day before, but Aunty Lee insisted on having the article read to her three times. Then she sent Nina to walk out to the 7-Eleven for the *Today* paper and told her, "You go online and look for me what the people are saying on STOMP!" (The Straits Times Online Mobile Print featured everything from shocking photos of highway accidents to rude service staff. It always had the latest news even if it was seldom accurate.)

The Lees had enrolled Nina in a basic computer course

within months of her arrival in the Lee household. M. L. Lee believed that people functioned satisfactorily only when they were constantly learning something, and Aunty Lee wanted somebody else's eyes and efforts to give her a shortcut into the whole new world of gossip she sensed e-buzzing around her. Despite her insistence on using traditional cooking methods, Aunty Lee loved new gadgets and technology. She might have an old charcoal brazier installed in the back alleyway and an old granite mortar and pestle that was never to be washed with soap, but she also had the latest model in blender-mixers (for catering) and her enormous state-of-the-art fridge, specially ordered from Germany, which had different compartments kept at different temperatures in the most energy-efficient way possible. So it was not surprising that Aunty Lee had a computer at home and an iPad 2 always close at hand, and Nina's skills and eyesight kept her connected with a planet of food and eaters.

And perhaps it pleased Aunty Lee, just a little, to know this irritated Selina, who said as often as she could, "If you want someone to look up things online, you can ask Mark. He's always fiddling around with his computer," and "If Nina has enough free time to play with an iPad, you should send her over to clean our place!" That second suggestion, not really a joke, had been repeated several times.

There could be no disputing how beautifully the Binjai Park bungalow was maintained and how Nina had set up and managed the home vegetable garden, where she grew enough vegetables to supply the house and enough *pandan, limau purut,* and chilis to supply the shop. In fact Selina had even approached Nina directly, saying that Aunty Lee wouldn't need a live-in helper for much longer and for her own sake she should start looking for more long-term employers. Being Selina, she had added that Nina should know better than to expect that any other employer would allow her the same liberties that Aunty Lee did. As Aunty Lee said when Nina told her about this, Selina meant well. Nina tried to remember this. But still she enjoyed looking up things for Aunty Lee, and enjoyed it even more when Selina was around.

"Go online and find out if they know who it is yet!"

"Ma'am, when the police find out they will say. Now is just people guessing only."

Contrary to what Selina believed, there was quite enough work for Nina under Aunty Lee's supervision. That morning she had already watered and trimmed the garden, prepared and washed up breakfast, and made the pot of lemongrass-and-ginger tea (from freshly harvested lemongrass) and was currently employed in tailing mung-bean sprouts or *tow gay.* Because Aunty Lee insisted on sprouting her own green beans, this was slightly more complicated. Rather than the uniformly slim straight sprouts you could find in the market or supermarket, her sprouts were twisted and contorted. But they were also lusciously plump and juicy. "Like women," Aunty Lee said. "The skinny ones all no taste." Nina thought it fortunate that Aunty Lee only said that in private—so far. It was the kind of comment Harry Sullivan would have leaped on to make one of his awkward jokes.

"You don't know. One of them may have guessed right!" Aunty Lee padded round the table and poked at the iPad. "Even now they may be arresting the murderers!"

"Aunty Lee! Your hands are wet! After you short-circuit it, then you know!"

Still, Nina preferred Aunty Lee like this in the mornings. In the weeks and months after M. L. Lee's death, she had been politely silent. No trouble to anyone, she had said little, eaten little, and—as Nina knew because she was herself a light sleeper—slept little. All night she had heard her employer's steady, sad steps going round and round the house. Down the stairs, around the living room, stopping at the door of the study, where her husband used to sit with his papers when he was alive, then back up the stairs . . . only to return again to repeat the same pattern. It would have been better, Nina thought, if only Aunty Lee could have cried and fallen apart, because then she could have helped put her back together again.

Even now she occasionally found Aunty Lee standing silently before one of the portraits of the late M. L. Lee. There was at least one in each room—here, facing them in the living/dining room, M. L. Lee sat regally, his wife behind him with one small plump hand on his shoulder. That had been taken on their tenth wedding anniversary.

They had not had so many years left together. There was also a smaller photograph of M. L. Lee with his first wife, Dimples Koh. Aunty Lee kept it there because Dimples was Mark and Mathilda's mother, but it was unlikely Mark noticed the photo and Mathilda wasn't in Singapore to see it. Nina had never seen Aunty Lee paused in thought in front of that particular photograph.

Just then the intercom from the gate sounded. Nina was startled. They were not expecting any deliveries that morning.

"Did you order anything, ma'am?" Singapore might be safe, but you still had to be careful. Even here there were probably people who would take advantage of a rich old woman alone in her house with a poor maid.

"No, no." Aunty Lee fluttered toward the door, obviously intending to examine their visitor in person.

"Aunty Lee, please wait. Let me find out who it is and what they want first . . ."

But then Nina saw the two uniformed policemen standing at their gate and the police car stopped behind them and knew she was not going to be the one asking the questions.

"Sorry to disturb you like this," one of the officers said. "I am Senior Staff Sergeant Salim and this is my colleague Officer Pang. We are looking for Mrs. Rosie Lee."

Nina was taken aback. Aunty Lee, on the other hand, looked delighted. "You must come in and sit down," she insisted. When the men hesitated, she added, "I am an old lady, I cannot stand up for long. You want to ask me questions, you must come in and sit down."

SSS Salim was the newly appointed officer in charge of the Bukit Tinggi Neighbourhood Police Post, which included Binjai Park in its jurisdiction. This was a quiet, mostly upmarket residential area with few problems. The main reason for having a neighborhood police post there was because of the presence of the Swiss embassy, the International Community School, the Canadian International School, the German European School, and the homes of some of the wealthiest residents in Singapore.

In fact this was a posting that managed to be simultaneously a dead end and a potential big break. Some officers might have been very happy with it. Others might view it as an opportunity to make valuable contacts for the future. SSS Salim Mawar was just trying to find his feet. Awarded the Singapore Police Force Overseas Scholarship, he had graduated from the National University of Singapore with a bachelor of law (honors) and almost immediately proceeded on to obtain his master's of philosophy in criminology and law from Cambridge University. This was his first official post since returning to Singapore. He was well aware (some had said it to his face in warning) that he was being groomed to be one of the token Malays in the leading party. He was also well aware many of the English-educated, middle-class Chinese in his homeland treated him as more of an outsider than he had been in England.

But even if he sometimes felt like an outsider, there was, as yet, no other place that Salim considered home, and until he found one, Singapore would have to do. And in Singapore he could physically blend into his surroundings—a definite advantage for a police investigator, which was still how Salim saw his job. His aide, Officer Pang, though Chinese (and speaking English, Mandarin, and Cantonese as well as a smattering of Malay and Hokkien) did not share this advantage. Sergeant Timothy Pang was too good-looking. Whenever he entered a space, old women forgot their age, young women forgot themselves, and even men were not immune. It was not Officer Pang's fault, of course. And SSS Salim found it very useful having Officer Pang around because just looking at him threw most people off balance.

SSS Salim was impressed by the neatly ordered living room he was shown in to. He sat down on the seat Aunty Lee indicated to him before she sat herself down on the other side of the little coffee table. Officer Pang remained standing by the door.

"What about your colleague?"

"He's all right. Mrs. Lee, you called our head office to say that a woman was missing—a Miss Laura Kwee?"

Aunty Lee threw a guilty look in Nina's direction. As SSS Salim followed the look, Nina kept her face impassive. She hoped the policeman would recognize that she had no control over her boss's actions and not hold her responsible.

"I only said maybe it's her—if you still don't know the identity of the body you found in the sea. But I have a new name for you now: Marianne Peters is also missing."

The two policemen exchanged glances. This time it was Officer Pang who answered.

"We have already received several calls concerning Marianne Peters. A friend of hers is concerned."

"And?"

"And we have spoken to her family, who assured us there is nothing to worry about. In fact her brother, who is an NMP, informed us she is out of Singapore, traveling with friends." It was clear from his tone that the word of a member of parliament, even if nominated rather than elected, was sacrosanct and therefore no further queries would be made.

"Oh yes, of course. That is what she said she was going to tell them. But do they know where she really is? Have they spoken to her? Can you ask them who are those friends she is supposed to be traveling with?"

SSS Salim dismissed Aunty Lee's suggestions with a vague gesture that could have meant either that he would get onto their trail as soon as this interview was over or that he didn't know and didn't care. This ability to be respectfully vague had served him very well throughout his studies and was proving useful within the force as well.

"It is Laura Kwee that we are concerned with right now, ma'am. Can you tell us how you know her? And how you came to believe that she was missing?"

Aunty Lee looked at him for a long moment. She was not refusing to answer, just studying him; SSS Salim got the feeling that she was reading his mind. In reality, Aunty Lee was engaged in putting together all the facts she had so far—including the appearance of a police vehicle at her doorstep—and also studying Officer Pang, who was standing soberly by the entrance.

"You aren't just here to follow up on my phone call," she said finally. "You came to tell me that Laura Kwee is dead."

The handsome policeman looked startled enough to confirm it.

"Of course we try to follow up on every tip we get," SSS Salim explained. "But most of the time it doesn't come to anything."

"This time it did!" In spite of the horror of the news, Aunty Lee was clearly fascinated by it. She waved to Nina and hot tea (ginseng and *Cordyceps* this time to strengthen them against the shock) was made and brought out for all of them along with some of Aunty Lee's peanut biscuits.

"What we want to ask you . . ." As SSS Salim spoke he nodded to Officer Pang, who produced a small recorder that he placed on the coffee table. This was obviously the start of the official interview. "What alerted you to the fact that Miss Kwee was missing?"

"But she was killed, wasn't she? Or are you not sure whether it's her? I don't think I have any photographs of Laura Kwee . . . Nina, can you look up Laura Kwee's Facebook page for the officers? Or would you like Nina to go with you to the mortuary to identify her body? I can come with you also, but my eyes are not so good already now."

"We are certain it is Miss Laura Kwee," SSS Salim cut in hurriedly before Nina could follow up on any of Aunty Lee's instructions. He was still calm and still authoritatively patient, but he was starting to show signs of the bemused stress that affected most people when they were first taken over by Aunty Lee. "I mean we are certain of her identity. We don't need to identify her. What I would like to know is what made you report her as missing."

"I read in the newspapers this morning that you were trying to identify the body that was found," Aunty Lee explained. "Or rather Nina read it to me. And yesterday already we heard it on the radio. So I thought I should help if I could."

"When did you phone, ma'am?" Nina usually had to dial the numbers for Aunty Lee.

"Yesterday. When you were at the back setting up the grill, before all the other people arrived," Aunty Lee admitted. "I didn't want to worry you. Nine-nine-nine is such an easy number to tap-tap-tap, I thought I would just take care of it without bothering you."

"None of her colleagues or family members reported her missing." SSS Salim was not to be diverted. "In fact, when we spoke to them, most of them said they thought she had gone off on holiday over Chinese New Year and taken leave to extend her trip. And when we checked—we found she had taken leave. So what alerted you to the fact that she was missing?"

Nina was beginning to feel irritated. Shouldn't these policemen be out running after whoever had killed Laura Kwee and thrown her into the sea rather than cross-examining Aunty Lee about her phone call?

"We didn't think that Laura Kwee is missing," Nina said. "In fact we were sure she was not missing because just before dinner last night she phoned Ma'am Selina to say she not coming."

This was of interest to both policemen. "You say last night someone called Selina says she got a phone call from Laura Kwee?" SSS Salim asked for the benefit of the recording even as Officer Pang glanced at his watch to carefully note the time this nugget of information had been handed to them. "Do you know what time this call came through? And can you tell me how to get in touch with this Selina? What is her full name?"

"Selina Lee. She's married to my late husband's son, Mark. You are trying to narrow down the time of death, right? Selina told us about the call around seven p.m. That means Laura Kwee must have phoned her earlier than that. That means she must have been killed between—" Aunty Lee stopped abruptly.

"You found a body yesterday morning," Aunty Lee began again. "You are saying that is the same body that you have now identified as Laura Kwee—even though Laura Kwee was alive yesterday evening."

"And that has probably been in the water for at least three days. That is why we would like to talk to Selina Lee," said SSS Salim.

"Ma'am Selina is going to be angry," Nina suggested after the two police officers left with their information. That was not saying much, given how often Selina found something to be angry about.

"I'm sure we'll hear all about that soon enough," Aunty Lee said. "Invite those two over for dinner tonight. Tell them I want to cook for them because they will be too tired after talking to the police. And then phone that Carla Saito for me. Tell her it is not the body of her friend Marianne, but I want her to come and talk to me. If she doesn't want to come here or go to the shop to talk to me, I will go to her hotel to talk to her there. Quick, do it now!"

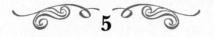

5

Carla Saito's Story

Carla Saito chose to meet Aunty Lee back at the café.

"Marianne didn't go diving with friends," she told Aunty Lee. "She just told her parents she was going to be with friends they knew so they wouldn't worry about her. She took extra time off work because she was going to spend time with me. We had a lot to talk about."

Marianne Peters and Carla Saito had met the year before when Marianne visited Washington for an IT conference. They had instantly clicked, despite being from such different backgrounds. Carla had shown Marianne around Washington. Even though it was not her hometown, she knew her way around better than Marianne, who was on her first visit to the States.

"And I know what you're going to say, but it wasn't just a holiday thing. We spent all our time together there; she skipped all her final sessions so that we could take a quick trip to the mountains. And after she went back to Singapore—I mean came back here—we talked every day on Skype—"

"You became very good friends very fast," Aunty Lee observed sweetly.

Carla Saito looked at her for a moment, but there was nothing but curiosity in Aunty Lee's expression.

"Yes, we did," Carla said quietly. "And we planned this for a long time. Me coming out here to join her, I mean. I had to sell my apartment and hand in my notice—"

"What do you do? For work, I mean."

"Well, to put it simply, I work with computers. I'm in IT security."

"But you can't go on staying at the Frangipani Inn. That kind of place is not good for a single girl staying alone. Why don't you come and stay at my house? I have a lot of room in my house. Nina, you can make the bed in the side room for her, right? You can have your own toilet, and then if you want to go and talk to Marianne's family tomorrow, you can walk over. They are just nearby, just further up the road and up the hill. If it's not too hot, you can easily walk. I can show you where to go or I can go with you. I know her parents very well."

"I don't know—"

"Don't worry." Aunty Lee sensed her alarm. "If you are happy in your room there, then that is fine."

"Well, it's not so bad. But the main thing is, Marianne booked the room for us. She put down the deposit and I just had to check in when I got here. She was going to meet me there so that we could talk. Plus it's cheap because it's a backpackers' haunt and nobody her family knows would ever go near there, so it was safe."

"You must be glad Marianne is all right," Aunty Lee said to Carla. "I mean now that you know she is not the body that they found."

"Of course I am. I just don't understand why, if she's all right—and why, if she could call someone else—she didn't call me."

Aunty Lee nodded, understanding. Even a tragedy was easier to understand than abandonment. "As long as there is life, there is hope," she said. "Tell me why you came here to look for Laura Kwee. How did you know that Marianne would get in touch with her about not coming?"

"I didn't. But Marianne told me Laura got her brother interested in this place and he got her and his wife to go too. And then there was some fuss at the first dinner, right? Laura was trying to match Marianne up with some guy? But Laura called her afterward and they talked and she explained things to her, and then she said Laura was getting someone to help us."

"Help you? What do you mean?"

Carla Saito shrugged. "I don't know. It was going to be some big surprise for me. All I know is she was pretty excited about it. She said we could have some time together to work things out in peace without really leaving Singapore. Anyway, I should be going. It's really late. Thank you very much. For the food and for listening."

"Would you like me to come with you to Marianne Peters's house and ask her mother where she is?"

"No! I mean there's no point. I know what she'll say. She thinks that Marianne is off on a travel vacation with friends. Marianne was only telling them that because she wanted us to have some time together. I don't want to tell them she was lying. If she comes back and finds out I told them she lied, she's going to be so mad."

"Then why not just meet her somewhere else? Why come to Singapore?"

"Because if we managed to figure out what we want to do, then we could have gone to tell her family together. I mean, if I managed to persuade her to see things my way," Carla Saito said quietly. "I wanted everything to be clear and open and honest from the beginning. This way, even if her family wasn't happy about it, at least they would know how we felt and what we wanted and they could take their time to come around to the idea—but they would never have to think that we lied to them. Of course, it didn't quite work out that way. Marianne said I didn't understand what traditional Asian parents were like."

"You have to tell her parents," Aunty Lee said. "They have a right to know Marianne is not away with her friends."

"No. I mean . . . just wait. Please. If she just took some time off to think about things and I've gone and talked to her parents—"

"If you don't want to talk to her parents, at least tell her brother. Mycroft is a nice boy. He won't say anything—"

Carla Saito shook her head. "No. I know all about Mycroft Peters. He's the worst of them all."

6

Family Dinner

Though she was far from convinced, Aunty Lee agreed not to say anything to Marianne's family—at least for the moment. In contrast to Carla Saito's relief to find out that Marianne was not the body found on Sentosa, the news left Aunty Lee feeling even more worried. There was a problem with the phone call no one else seemed to have noticed. If Laura Kwee had already been murdered, how could Marianne have left a message with her? And if the message had not come from Laura, why had Marianne been mentioned at all unless . . .

Aunty Lee did not want to follow that thought through till she was forced to. Fortunately having Selina and Mark come to dinner provided ample distraction.

For once Selina was paying more attention to her own plate than what Mark was or was not eating. And she was eating Aunty Lee's food with gusto. Mark watched his wife helping herself to sambal squid and black-bean fish without a word about cholesterol and preservatives, and helped himself as well. It was about time Selina had a good meal without worrying about what she was eating. It seemed as though being questioned by the police had improved both her mood and her appetite.

Aunty Lee had been half afraid that Selina would blame her for talking to the police. But Selina was surprisingly good-natured about the experience. She and Mark had had to go to the Bukit Tinggi Police Post for an interview with SSS Salim and had spent almost four hours there.

"I told them I had no idea whatsoever that Laura was missing. I expected her to turn up like we arranged, she texted me to say sorry she couldn't make it—that's all I knew. But they kept asking all these questions about how well I knew Laura, had she said anything about boyfriends or stalkers—and they took my phone. I think they are going to try to trace where her text came from. All I can say is they better get it back to me soon! What am I going to do without a phone—I'm running a business, you know! What if my clients try to call me?"

"I blame SingTel," Mark said. "I told them, sometimes messages don't get through until hours later."

"But actually answering their questions didn't take so long," Selina continued. "Yes, give me just a bit more rice,

Nina—they wrote down all our answers in first person as though we wrote them down ourselves, and frankly speaking, their English isn't very good. But I wasn't going to sign my name on the statement until they got it right."

"Sel gave them an English lesson," Mark commented. "I said they should just have let us write our own statements, they could read them over, and that would be that." Mark looked tired and more stressed than his wife. But then he had never liked confrontations.

"I did not," Selina said. "But they said I was very helpful— that we were very helpful. They didn't know about that woman coming to look for Laura that night."

"Carla Saito didn't come to look for Laura. She was trying to find Marianne Peters," Aunty Lee pointed out.

"That's not true. When she came in she was asking for Laura Kwee. Anyway, the police aren't interested in Marianne. Marianne isn't even missing, she's away on holiday. That woman came in and asked for Laura Kwee. We all heard her. You heard her, didn't you, Aunty Lee? Why didn't you tell the police about her? They were very interested in how to get hold of her, so I told them I thought I heard her say she was staying at the Frangipani. I think they're going to talk to her too."

Something in the way Selina said this made Nina wonder what exactly she had told the police about Carla Saito. Aunty Lee could guess. She changed the subject.

"I wonder whether this is going to change the way people see Sentosa. It can't be very good for the resort there."

"I remember going to Sentosa during school holidays," Mark said, surprising his stepmother. "I remember the mangrove swamps. Dad had a friend who was crazy about the mangrove swamps. Uncle Bian said they were like natural water filters. Can you imagine, he did his thesis on wave patterns in artificial mangrove swamps."

Aunty Lee was uncharacteristically quiet during the meal. Nina recognized it as her analyzing mode; the one that appeared when she was trying to reverse engineer a dish or when she was trying to decide whether some variation in taste was good or bad.

"They refused to say if poor Laura was definitely murdered," Mark said. "I asked if they had any leads or any suspects, but they wouldn't say." Talking about murder and suspects came naturally enough, thanks to forensic crime thrillers on cable television.

Selina usually put a damper on gruesome speculations, but now she said, "But you can see they think it is murder, don't they? And the worst thing is—I think they took my phone because I may have been the last person Laura talked to!"

The concentration on Aunty Lee's face grew deeper, if possible. She stared at the unfinished rice on her plate, but Nina knew she was really trying to untangle events. Nina could guess what was on Aunty Lee's mind. Though SSS Salim had not told them how long Laura Kwee had been dead, it was clear that her body had been found before

Selina received that last text from her. The same thought had occurred to Mark.

"If it wasn't a SingTel glitch," he said, "it might have been the murderer that sent you that message. Laura was already dead yesterday evening, you know. They said she's probably been dead for at least a week."

"Don't be ridiculous," Selina said. "They said they couldn't be certain of the time of death. Anyway, the message was definitely from Laura. She signed off with that silly smiley face she always uses. The phone must have been out of range or something. You know how sometimes messages just don't go through until hours after you send them?"

Aunty Lee looked up and saw Nina watching her. "You can clear my plate," she said. "There are ways to track mobile phones these days, right? Go and ask that nice staff sergeant are they tracking Laura's phone."

"I am sure he is already doing that, ma'am." Nina deftly cleared Aunty Lee's half-eaten dinner plate. That there was food left over was an indication of how concerned Aunty Lee was. "Ma'am, don't worry. The police will know what to do."

After Mark and Selina left, Aunty Lee continued brooding.

"What is the matter, ma'am?"

"That message didn't come from Laura. Whoever it was wanted to make people think Laura was still alive.

What I'm worried about is why did the message mention Marianne—but no need to go into all that. Go and phone that nice staff sergeant or that handsome young assistant of his and tell him that you heard a phone ringing somewhere outside the shop but you could not find it."

The excitement of giving a statement to the police was not all that was making Selina happy that night. Mark had finally read the piece in the *Island High Life* reviewing the recent wine dining at Aunty Lee's Delights. "They don't mention the wine at all," Mark said, peeved, but Selina thought he should have been glad. After all, the writer of the article had not been impressed by Aunty Lee's supposedly classy food—the anonymous reviewer made fun of the fact that dinner had been served on two-dollar Daiso plates. Selina had complained about those plates repeatedly, but Aunty Lee had done nothing, saying no one noticed such things. Well, that was no longer true.

"I tried to get her to read it because of the plates. But you know what she's like. You should bring it up. She has to change those plates now if she doesn't want to be a laughingstock."

"Sel, you didn't write that comment, did you?" Mark asked.

"Don't be stupid, of course I didn't. But print it out for me, okay? I want to show it to Aunty Lee. And make it large print. She won't admit how bad her eyesight is and I suspect Nina only reads her what she wants to hear."

She had to repeat this twice before Mark answered, and even then he only said, "Maybe."

"What's wrong with you? If you go on like that, people are going to suspect there was something going on between you and Laura Kwee!" It was not clear from her tone whether this was a joke or a threat.

Mark knew his wife. One of her rules of life was not to make threats she was not prepared to follow up on.

7

Putting Information Together

Over the next few days the grisly details about the body on Sentosa were released to the public via the press and the Internet. Aunty Lee read the papers herself repeatedly, with her magnifying glass, as though afraid Nina would miss something, and she asked Nina to start accounts with all the online news and gossip sites so that Aunty Lee was kept up-to-date with speculations and possible sightings.

The few facts were unpleasant. Laura Kwee's body had been found wrapped in a plastic bag. Her body might have been in the seawater for up to a week—or more. It was hard to say exactly. She had died of suffocation and traces of drugs had been found in her system.

This last information had not come from the newspapers. It was not for nothing that Aunty Lee had been married to a man who had donated enough money to the Singapore General Hospital (where the postmortem was performed) to have a wing of that institution named after him. Aunty Lee had made a few social calls, asked a few curious questions . . . and been told the drug found in Laura Kwee's system was ketamine.

Nina had looked up the details for her. "'Ketamine is used as an anesthetic for both humans and animals,'" she read off her iPad. "'These days it is used more on animals, and in America and Australia, veterinary clinics get broken into for their supplies. It is banned in Singapore but still surfaces occasionally as "Vitamin K" or "Kit Kat." It is more commonly found in Hong Kong, the United States, and Australia, where it is the drug of choice at dance parties or raves because it produces a state of dreamy intoxication that lasts for an hour or less.'"

"An hour or less," Aunty Lee repeated. "That is better than getting drunk, right? Why is it banned here when they still allow people to get drunk and drive cars? Are there side effects? Does it cause cancer?"

"There are other bad effects, ma'am. It can cause memory problems and it can make some people react aggressively or violently."

"Again no different from people going and getting drunk, what!"

Nina speed-read on. Facts were facts but she didn't like the conclusion Aunty Lee was drawing so far. It was not safe in Singapore for anyone—even old ladies—who thought drugs were not dangerous. Though in Aunty Lee's case, she was more likely to have trouble with the authorities than with addiction.

" 'It is dangerous because you can feel drunk even if you have not touched any alcohol. You may lose your sense of time and identity and think you are having out-of-body experiences. People use it as a date-rape drug because it is very fast acting. People have said the last thing they re-member is having a drink, then everything after that is blurry.' "

"Still doesn't sound so different from people getting drunk," Aunty Lee said stubbornly. "You should hear some of the things people say when they have been drinking too much. Not only the men. The women, maybe because they are less used to drinking in public, can be much, much worse!"

Nina shook her head. She had real work to do—there was always something that needed to be done in the house or in the shop. People who came in and said how beautifully organized everything was did not realize that maintaining things in the right places, functioning and dust-free, was a full-time nonstop job. And that was before factoring in a busybody old lady who was always bringing home strange things and stranger people just because they had caught her interest. Not for the first time Nina thought wistfully of a nursing job where her off time was hers alone. But she knew she would not leave the café if she were given the chance. Even if Singapore was not home to her, Aunty Lee was definitely family.

Nina slid one of the cutlery drawers off its rails and carried it into the living room. This was where she usually took care of noncooking chores because while she worked she could answer Aunty Lee's questions and read her anything required.

"Would you take this Vitamin K or Kit Kat?" Auntie Lee asked suddenly.

"No, ma'am. Of course not. I'm not crazy. These things are bad for you."

"Why do you think Laura Kwee took it, then? She didn't drink much. She wasn't even used to wine. You remember how she behaved at the first dinner?"

Of course Nina remembered. Laura Kwee had tasted all the wine in all her glasses before realizing Mark meant to walk the guests through the samples one by one. Seated between Mycroft Peters and Harry Sullivan, Laura had chattered to both of them till, rebuffed by Mycroft, who fixed his attention firmly on Mark (Mycroft took wine seriously—but then Mycroft took most things seriously), she had focused on Harry, who, himself, was leaning across to whisper to Marianne, who was seated on his other side. Laura had reminded Nina of a schoolgirl trying to get a boy's attention. She had waved to Nina and asked her to top up her glasses. Nina got no direction from Mark or Selina, who were deliberately ignoring Laura. Laura, getting impatient, waved two of her already empty glasses in the air. She knew she was not drunk. After all, Mark had assured her that people never got drunk at wine tastings. She was just slightly tipsy and feeling daring and sophisticated . . .

"Do you remember what Laura said to Marianne that night?" Aunty Lee's thoughts had obviously run along the same lines as Nina's. "Something about her supposed holiday plans? And I could see Marianne was quite cross with her. Do you know what she was talking about?"

Nina had no idea. All she remembered was Aunty Lee calling her to the pantry and passing her a bottle of red wine to top up Laura's glasses.

"The same in all the glasses?" Nina had been concerned. Mark had been very particular earlier about not getting his special wines and the sequence of glasses mixed up. What Aunty Lee handed her was one of the bottles kept in the kitchen for adding body to soups and sauces.

"She won't be able to tell the difference."

In retrospect, it had probably been a bad idea. But at the time their only concern had been to keep Laura satisfied and quiet. Instead she had gone on giggling and whispering, rolling her eyes when Mark glared and Selina shushed her. Laura had definitely not been used to wine. Selina had been so furious with the woman that Nina would not have been surprised if Laura had been banned from all future wine dining events. But apparently Laura had apologized abjectly, offered to help at future wine tastings (for free), and been forgiven.

Laura Kwee had not struck Aunty Lee as the sort of person to experiment with drugs. In her thirties, she had been a secondary school teacher until she gave it up for a career in arts management. She had probably hoped that the change would lead to meeting exciting people and becoming or marrying an arts impresario, but so far her life had plodded on without any sign of taking off.

Laura Kwee had always seemed a safe, responsible, rather dull woman to Nina. Overly concerned with what other people thought of her perhaps. And overly disappointed with how little most did. Several times she had tried to get Nina to tell her what Aunty Lee and Mark "really" thought of her. It had been easy for Nina to say honestly that she had never heard Laura's name mentioned.

"Maybe someone gave it to her? Put it in her drink or something?"

Things like that happened on television, but it was hard to imagine it happening in Singapore, and to someone like Laura Kwee. It was not just the difficulty of imagining Laura Kwee in a nightclub partying and drinking, but why Laura Kwee? Why would someone have picked her?

"I have to talk to that girl again. That American girl," Aunty Lee said. "You wrote down her hotel and mobile phone, right?"

"Ma'am, if you don't know what is happening, how can she know? That Carla Saito just arrived in Singapore, she never met Laura Kwee before."

"But there's something she knows and wouldn't say. I

could see it very clearly. I just didn't want to push her with everybody around. And those Cunninghams are also not saying something. I could see it from how they reacted to her when she came in. Maybe it's the drug connection. Maybe they were Laura's drug connection. You heard them say they came to meet her too, right?"

"You can ask Senior Staff Sergeant Salim about the drugs," Nina said, seeing a familiar car pull up outside the gate. "But careful—he'll think you want to take drugs to go party!"

"I doubt he'll tell me. Anyway, he may not approve of us knowing such things." Aunty Lee stopped and looked around, nose twitching slightly as though she were trying to detect an elusive scent. Her hearing and eyesight might be failing, but she could still read people better than most. The change in Nina's attention had alerted her.

"What is it? Is somebody here? Who is it? Not that policeman again?" Without looking out her front windows, Aunty Lee deduced the arrival of SSS Salim before he had time to buzz the gate intercom. She perked up immediately.

"That's good. Maybe he can answer some of my questions. Let him in, Nina. Put him in the living room and give him a drink. I have to go and change my clothes."

The automatic gate clicked open and SSS Salim walked up the short stretch of gravel driveway that led up to the house. This time he was able to take in details he missed on his previous visit with all his thoughts focused on the dead woman. A lane branched off, leading around and behind the house—to a garage, Salim presumed, since he could not see any cars. The staff sergeant stopped at the steps leading to the glassed-in verandah. It was clearly designed to be enjoyed in air-conditioning. This was how the rich lived in equatorial heat: enjoying green lushness within a space of air-conditioned comfort.

Salim took a deep breath to prepare himself. He was not intimidated by the rich. In his opinion, having money did not make you a better or worse person. But in his experience, while the very wealthy and the very poor were relaxed in their dealings with others, those in between could be more difficult to deal with. They were very conscious of trying to climb into what they saw as the upper class and very afraid of sliding down into the lower. They were also generally very eager to show how well they knew their rights by being unhelpful and rude to a police officer who was just trying to do his job. SSS Salim had asked his aide to wait in the car so that it could be moved immediately if anyone had to go in or out. Some people also leaped at the chance of reporting police vehicles every opportunity they got. SSS Salim did not really mind that either. It kept his men on their toes, making them more vigilant. But it also meant a lot of time spent on paperwork and he had other problems to deal with right then.

"Please come in and take a seat. Aunty will be coming soon. You want to drink coffee or tea or soft drink?"

Again his presence seemed to have been anticipated,

but SSS Salim didn't mind. He had noticed the maid from his previous visit hovering protectively around her mistress. Most people did not bother to notice maids and cleaners, likewise drivers and technicians, but these were the people Salim had grown up with. Salim also remembered this woman because she had not struck him as a domestic helper at first—or even a waitress—though she had been waiting on Aunty Lee. Was it her posture? Her clothes? SSS Salim could not say. Her manner as she welcomed him into the house now was faultless, as it had been a few days ago.

"Thank you," SSS Salim said. He hesitated.

"Sir, no need to take off shoes," the girl said.

She was very good at reading people, SSS Salim thought. Had he been on a private visit, he would likely have removed his shoes nonetheless. But today SSS Salim was calling on Mrs. M. L. Lee on official business and the Singapore police force did not take off its shoes for anybody.

The living room was large and airy. On the walls, modern white curving shelves undulated above stolid pieces of heavily inlaid teak furniture. SSS Salim was no expert in old furniture, but he guessed these were antiques and probably expensive. He sat down. The sofa seemed to be made of bamboo, but the thick green seat was comfortably cushioned. Overall, the room had an effect of lightness above and solidity beneath. Somewhat to his surprise, Salim immediately felt comfortable there.

"You work in the café also?" Salim asked the maid. The

question would have sounded purely conversational to anyone unfamiliar with Singapore's Ministry of Manpower rule that stated that a foreign domestic helper "shall not engage in any form of employment, paid or unpaid, other than that of a Domestic Helper."

Nina was only too aware that Aunty Lee could be fined and she herself deported if this man decided to make trouble. Even as she decided she didn't like him, Nina knew she could not let him see she did not like him. She gave him a wide, shy smile that could have meant anything.

"How long have you been working in Singapore?"

"Sir, I like work in Singapore very much!" Nina beamed to make up for the abrupt deterioration of her spoken English.

SSS Salim looked at her suspiciously, but before he could say anything further, they heard the chair lift descending the stairs. The chair lift that followed the curve of the specially constructed staircase had been installed after the late M. L. Lee broke his ankle in a golf accident. Normally it was used only to transport Aunty Lee's enormous ornamental flowerpots between floors. But Aunty Lee knew how to make an appearance and did so now.

Even Nina, who knew her better than anyone alive, was taken aback. Earlier Aunty Lee had been perfectly presentable in her usual work-at-home outfit of a comfortable T-shirt and what she called her tai chi trousers. Now she was wearing a coarse, dark blue silk blouse over loose natural linen trousers. She was also wearing her pearls.

"How nice to see you again, Sergeant," Aunty Lee greeted SSS Salim graciously. To her, comfort meant being dressed for the job. It was obvious to her that getting the upper hand in an interview with a police officer required a different outfit from supervising the cleaning of bean sprouts.

Nina remained in her typical at-home attire—today she was wearing a light pink T-shirt beneath a flowered sundress. It was Aunty Lee who had come up with this compromise after Selina declared the sundresses Aunty Lee had bought for Nina (so cheap, so comfortable, after they wear out you can use them for cleaning or patchwork) not suitable for a maid. Her chief objection had been to the strappy top and bare shoulders, which would catch the attention of men and boyfriends and lead to rape, pregnancy, abortions, and other such expense-causing phenomena. Selina was firmly convinced that how women dressed, talked, and behaved was to blame for unwanted male attention.

But now Aunty Lee did not depend solely on her appearance. Right now she was playing the grande dame, very different from the busy café chef.

"How nice to see you again, Senior Staff Sergeant. Do take a seat if you haven't come to arrest me. You haven't? Oh good.

"I gather you are here about the body on Sentosa. Such a terrible place. I still remember stories about dead bodies washing up on the beach there in the morning after the

Japanese took Chinese men and boys out on boats at night. They tied them together before they shot them and threw them in, so that even if they didn't die right away from the bullets, they would drown. Of course, at that time it was just a Malay fishing kampong there. And the Malay villagers would secretly bury the bodies, and even years later, when the wives and mothers and sisters came to ask, they could tell them where their men were buried. Did you know that? It is part of our history, how an outside threat made different races here watch out for each other. But nowadays people are not interested in that, they only want to know about property values."

That was rich, Salim thought, coming from someone whose District 10 property was probably among the highest valued on the island. But he appreciated Aunty Lee's attempt to establish a connection with him. And he wanted information from her too, so he responded in kind.

"My uncles used to tell us about that time when they brought us fishing as kids. Every school holiday we used to look forward to going out on the boats. From Pasir Panjang right across to Sentosa. For us it was just fun. And sometimes when we went out night fishing, we would try to scare each other. But my uncles always told us to respect the dead."

"Speaking of the dead," Aunty Lee said, now that tea had arrived and her welcome accepted. "Are you here to talk about Laura Kwee's cell phone?"

"Laura Kwee's cell phone was found in a burning bin outside your shop." SSS Salim got straight to the point.

"The red metal one below the flowerpots?"

"Yes. Mrs. Lee, I would like to ask you to help us by telling me who was present at your café that night. We are interviewing all the proprietors along that stretch."

"Wait, wait. Slow down for me, young man. You say you found Laura Kwee's phone in the burning bin—you were looking for it there? Why?"

Nina was impressed anew by Aunty Lee's acting skills. But then again, she might not have been acting. She genuinely wanted to know why the police were following up on this particular tip, given the many others she had called in.

"Yes, ma'am. It was fortunate that Laura Kwee had previously downloaded the GPS tracking application onto her phone. We knew that Mrs. Mark Lee received a text message from Laura Kwee's cell phone before the dinner that night. Therefore we know her phone had to be turned on so that the stolen-phone recovery application could work. Normally a mobile phone can only be traced when it is still on because the lookout servers need to be able to trigger the phone to use its GPS chip to determine the phone's location. This is the case with all stolen-cell-phone recovery programs. However, we were able to get enough information off the servers to be able track its approximate location at the time the message was sent."

SSS Salim spoke as though this elaborate system was

just a matter of course, but it was clear to Nina that he expected her and Aunty Lee to be impressed. Though she was impressed, Aunty Lee was focusing on something else.

"Wait, wait, wait a minute. That means that when I am carrying my hand phone, then you can track to where I am whether it is on or off?"

"Oh no, ma'am. Your phone has to be on so that it can use the servers or GPS to figure out where it is."

"But you managed to find Laura Kwee's phone even though it was off—unless it was still on?"

"No, no. That is different altogether. Because it is a crime investigation—"

"That means actually you can track whoever you want, but only the police are allowed to do it?"

Aunty Lee seemed genuinely curious. SSS Salim had encountered many hostile civilians and didn't think she was one of them.

"If I lose my phone, can you use that tracking system to find it for me?"

SSS Salim decided to get the conversation back on track. "Probably not, madam. The reason why I came to see you today is to tell you that though we found the phone, the SIM card had been removed. We would like to take a look inside your shop to see if we can find it there."

"Why do you think you will find it there?"

"It is one of several locations we are searching, ma'am.

"Someone in the vicinity of the shop must have sent that

message and left the phone there," SSS Salim continued as though Aunty Lee had not spoken. "We would like to know who was there that night as well as how we can contact them."

Aunty Lee nodded to herself. SSS Salim looked at her, then in Nina's direction. Had he said too much too fast? He reminded himself that Mrs. Lee was an old lady. Worse, she was an important old lady. Salim had already been told to be "sensitive" in dealing with her and had thought that coming to see her in person was the way to be sensitive.

Nina was not concerned—at least not for Aunty Lee. She knew that look. Aunty Lee was processing. When she was ready she would—

"Do you need to get a search warrant to check my shop?"

Again Salim did not sense hostility.

"If necessary, I will have to get one. But I thought that if we can come to an agreement, then you can give us permission to look around your shop, and if we find anything, then we will take it from there."

SSS Salim did not want to frighten the woman by putting it too bluntly, but—

"You say Laura Kwee was already dead at the time when the message was sent. That means you don't think Laura sent the message from my shop. You think that the murderer sent it, right?"

"Well, we must not jump to any conclusions—"

"That means you think that one of the people who was there in my shop was the murderer who made the call! Nina! Nina!"

"Yes, ma'am?"

"Go and get the paper for him. You know the one we made that night with all the people and where they were around the time when Silly-Nah got the message . . ."

Now it was Aunty Lee's turn to look modestly efficient. SSS Salim was impressed. He was even more impressed when Nina returned with the list.

Mrs. Rosie Lee—*front shop, dining room, kitchen, pantry, outdoor cooking area (behind kitchen).*

Nina Balignasay—*dining room, kitchen, pantry, outdoor cooking area.*

Mark Lee—*dining room. Made several trips out to his car to get things he had forgotten.*

Selina Lee—*sidewalk, front shop. Used her mobile phone to text and call.*

Harry Sullivan—*sidewalk. Stayed outside till last minute smoking because no smoking inside, dining room.*

Frank and Lucy Cunningham—*front shop, dining room, toilet, Lucy Cunningham was texting, Frank Cunningham went out front and back to take photographs.*

Cherril Lim-Peters—*dining room, went to car several times with Mark Lee.*

> **Carla Saito**—*outside somewhere. She said that*
> *she came looking for Laura Kwee and had come*
> *straight in as soon as she arrived, but in fact*
> *she arrived much earlier and was watching from*
> *outside.*

The contact numbers for all these people were written down in Nina's careful script on the reverse side of the paper.

SSS Salim was very impressed. People were always coming up with ideas and suggestions on how he could do his work better, but they seldom passed him anything he could use, and even when they did, it was never so organized. In fact Aunty Lee's list reminded him of an ingredient list for one of his grandmother's recipes; written out casually but carefully.

"How do you know that?" SSS Salim asked, pointing to the comments that appeared after Carla Saito's name. "Did you see her outside? What was she doing?"

"Oh no. I didn't see her outside. If I had, of course I would have asked her to come in!"

"Then how do you know she hadn't just arrived?"

"We didn't hear a taxi. And she was sweaty but breathing slowly. As though she had been standing still in the heat for some time, not like somebody who had just walked in from the main road. And when she came inside to talk to us, I could see that right away she was looking at the women to see which of them was Laura Kwee. That showed that she didn't know who Laura Kwee was and that she already knew how many women were in the room. Therefore she must have been watching for some time, to know who came in."

All that made sense. "Thank you. I will keep it in mind," SSS Salim said.

"But you shouldn't waste time suspecting her," Aunty Lee said firmly. "Why I want you to take note of her now is because if Carla Saito was outside the shop for a while, she might have noticed whoever put the phone into the burning bin—if that's when they did it."

A police officer in most other countries would probably have dismissed this (politely or not) as the view of an old woman who knew nothing. But SSS Salim was a Singaporean before he was a policeman and he had been brought up by a grandmother who had kept him all too well aware that systems were most efficiently run on the experience of those who had been running them the longest. He also knew it was vital to differentiate facts from prejudice.

"Do you think the phone was put there at some other time? Not right after the text was sent? Why?"

"Because that fat Australian man always likes to stand there and smoke until the last minute. He always puts his cigarette butts inside the bin. I don't know how he can still taste my food after all that smoke. But if anybody put the phone in, then he would have seen, right? Afterward also, he didn't go off right away. He went to smoke there again."

"That's not very respectful," SSS Salim said.

Aunty Lee laughed. "Don't worry. I expect the ghosts can enjoy burned cigarettes as much as they enjoy burned paper money." Then, as a thought struck her, she looked sober again. "It's the attitude that matters, right? Not what you give to the dead but what you want to give them."

SSS Salim saw the old woman's maid look alarmed. But it seemed to him purely the alarm of a nursemaid concerned that the child she was looking after was toddling into the path of danger. There were portraits of an august-looking gentleman all over the house—both alone and with Aunty Lee—but no other sign of him. Still, the presence and positioning of those portraits said more about how the man was remembered than any amount of flowers and joss sticks could have done.

"I will have to send someone to take your statement formally," SSS Salim told Aunty Lee. "Thank you. You have been very helpful. If you don't mind, I will keep this paper, and if you give us permission to examine your shop space, we will be very careful—"

"Keep it, keep it. I have my own copy." Aunty Lee dismissed the paper. "You can come and look around my shop, but you won't find anything. If anything was left there, Nina would have found it already. Nina can find anything. But come, we can all go down and look now. I want you to show me where you found the phone."

As Aunty Lee started off, Nina gave SSS Salim a sympathetic look.

"Your boss is very energetic, eh?" Salim said.

"Slowly, slowly you will get used to her," Nina said. She waited for Salim to go after Aunty Lee, then followed them both out. "You don't suspect her, do you?"

"We have to suspect everybody. Tell me, are you familiar with the other members of your boss's family?"

Something in the way he said this made Nina pay attention. "Who are you asking about? Why?"

"The phone. There are ways of tracing calls and messages that I am not at liberty to discuss. But several of the messages on Laura Kwee's phone came from the phone belonging to Mrs. Lee's stepson, Mark. And there was a message from him telling her there was no need for her to come back." He paused and Nina waited.

"Sometimes there are things that family members do not notice or cannot say," Salim said. "But if you notice anything . . ." It was his turn to wait.

"I don't know anything," Nina said firmly. She held the door open for him.

Suddenly it was important to him to let her know that he was not just a policeman following routine.

"Very nice plants," he said. Then, feeling that this had sounded lame, he added, "I can't keep plants alive. Everything I try to grow dies."

"You are worried about Marianne Peters, aren't you?" Aunty Lee was standing in the driveway. Officer Pang had gotten out of the car and had positioned himself between her and the gate. He looked as though he was not sure if he would be called to stop her should the old lady decide to make a run for it.

"Whoever sent that message didn't know whether it was Laura's body you people found. Let's say it was whoever killed the poor woman and threw her into the sea. Obviously he was hoping the body would not be identified and wanted to throw you off the scent. But why would he add that Marianne said she wouldn't be there? Did he throw more than one body into the sea off Sentosa? That's what you're thinking, isn't it?"

"Ma'am," said SSS Salim. "I cannot comment on that."

The way he spoke told Aunty Lee that if he had not thought of the possibility she'd just suggested, he would certainly be considering it now, but she felt little triumph. Carla Saito might seem relieved that it was not Marianne's body that had surfaced, but Aunty Lee felt she would not be comfortable till she saw Marianne in person. There was still something Carla Saito was hiding. And even if Carla did not want to tell her what this was, Aunty Lee would have to get it out of her somehow.

In the meantime . . .

"You should speak to Marianne Peters's family. Find out more about this holiday she's supposed to have gone on. I'm not saying they have anything to do with the murder, but it seems very strange that they seem to have no worries at all about not hearing from Marianne!"

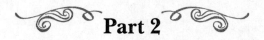

Part 2

Middle

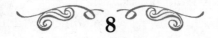

8

Waiting for Police Interviews

It was a pleasant enough room. Rectangular with a row of seats facing a long counter, it could have been the waiting area of a neighborhood dentist. But it was not. The Bukit Tinggi Neighbourhood Police Post was not where the Cunninghams had expected to be spending any of their time in Singapore. But Frank and Lucy were making the best of it. Lucy caught up on her e-mail and daily Bible verses on her MacBook Air while Frank took photographs of the station. The officer behind the counter looked uncomfortable but did not try to stop him. However, when Frank pointed the camera in her direction, she said, "No, no, cannot."

"It's just for a souvenir," Frank Cunningham said. "To show where we've been."

"No, sorry, sir. Photo taking is not allowed."

"Frank, don't bother the poor woman," Lucy said without looking up from her reading.

"In case you're never seen again, they don't want any proof you've been here!" Harry Sullivan said. He laughed to show that he was joking, but his laughter was not very convincing. It was plain to the Cunninghams, and probably to the police officer as well, that Harry was not happy about where he was.

The neighborhood police post was not an unpleasant place to be waiting. At least there was air-conditioning. Despite her son's tirades against power consumption and global warming, Lucy Cunningham felt like a functioning human only in an air-conditioned room. And the nice officer had told her she was welcome to plug her computer into the station's outlet, so she was quite content to catch up on her reading and e-mails. Traveling with Frank had left her very little time on her own. He didn't like to see her sitting quietly because he thought she would worry and brood about the matter that was looming so painfully over both of them. Frank knew that getting anxious about how things might work out never changed anything. But knowing this didn't always stop the worrying, and that was why anything, even this local inconvenience, was a welcome distraction. But though she appreciated Frank's good intentions, Lucy sometimes wished they could talk about it.

She wanted to wallow and be miserable, even if it did not help. She wished she could let herself go and have a good cry, but she did not want to upset Frank, so she went on reading the selected Bible verses on her little computer.

"How long do you think this will go on?" Harry Sullivan asked. "I mean, we didn't even know the poor girl; it's nothing to do with us!"

"You met her, didn't you? What was she like?" Harry might just have been venting his frustration but Frank Cunningham was always ready to talk.

"Not a real good looker. A bit too much flesh on her, but she knew how to dress to catch a man's eye, if you get what I mean. If you ask me, that's what got her into trouble. She was looking for the wrong sort of attention and she found it."

Frank Cunningham nodded. He knew the type. "I'm okay with women dressing to please themselves. That said, some girls today forget there is also the need to dress appropriately because of how others will see you. Otherwise they'll just attract sex predators and perverts."

"Hear, hear," Harry Sullivan agreed.

Frank Cunningham warmed to him and to his subject.

"Look, from an honest man's point of view, if a woman dresses like a slut, the probability of her getting sexually assaulted rises, am I right? We call ourselves civilized, but the animal, carnal nature of man is still very real today and you cannot deny sexual attractions are for real. So how a woman dresses does affect the probability of attack. Here we're not discounting her right to dress as she pleases. It is her safety we're concerned about. Talk all you like about women's rights, we can't fight sinful human nature!"

Harry Sullivan was a bit put out by the tirade he had unwittingly unleashed. He looked at Lucy Cunningham, whose attention remained fixed on her computer. Apparently this kind of outburst was nothing unusual for Frank.

"Then you support women wearing head scarves and long skirts?" the police officer behind the desk asked conversationally. Frank looked at her with some suspicion. She was in uniform, of course. He could not tell what race she was, but she was not wearing a head scarf.

"If you are married, then as long as your husband accepts how you dress, you won't go wrong. Don't get me wrong, miss. I believe women have the right to wear what they want. Except there is this reality check a woman needs to understand. Psychologically a man is attracted by what he sees, which leads to arousal and to desire. It's in the male DNA, they can't help it."

"No matter what a woman is wearing, sexual assault is a criminal offense," the officer said, still in a neutral conversational tone.

Harry Sullivan had dropped out of the conversation and was pointedly reading public information posters on the wall. Perhaps Frank Cunningham was hoping to reclaim his new friend's attention when he raised his voice slightly and continued.

"Officer, if you read *The Naked Ape* by Desmond Morris, who is an eminent anthropologist, you'll see he says that civilized man has lost his sense of smell. Nowadays sexual arousal is activated by sight. Women are aroused by emotion and touch, so they don't understand such things. Wearing head scarves doesn't help because that is also a trigger. When a woman is completely covered, the mystery excites the man's imagination like the forbidden fruit syndrome. My point here is that 'don't tempt the man' should apply."

"Should women dress like men, then? Do away with temptation?"

Lucy Cunningham looked up when the officer said this. She recognized the trigger and hoped Frank was not going to go off on another of his tirades, not in a police station in a foreign country, but—

"Even the public restroom doors use the symbol of a man in pants and a woman in a dress," Frank Cunningham said. "If you have women dressed as men, everybody is going to get confused about everything! Pants-wearing women will soon forget how to act like ladies!" He looked toward the desk.

By now the police officer was intently studying a pamphlet on volunteering for the neighborhood watch and refusing to meet his eye.

"You tell what's in a book by its cover, and in the same way you can see what is in a woman by how she dresses. If you dress like a man, you disgrace your husband and dishonor the name of Jesus. It is these pants-wearing women that kindle the fire of adultery in the hearts of men!"

Lucy wanted to warn her husband that there were probably Buddhists and Muslims and other heathens listening, but she said nothing. There was no point. Her husband lived his whole life as a good man should and nothing she said would change him, because by his definition, good men were not guided by their wives.

Seeing his words go unchallenged, Frank looked disappointed.

"Short-haired women in pants . . . it's just not right."

Harry Sullivan gave him a wink. "If you'd seen that other missing girl—Marianne Peters—you could have given her some advice there. All you ever saw her in was pants. Don't think she even owned a skirt. But short-haired or not, you couldn't mistake her for a guy! Do you have daughters back home?"

"No. Only a son."

"Well, that's easier, isn't it?" Harry said. He was taken aback by the look in the other man's eyes—impossible to tell whether it was pain or rage, but whichever it was, it was strong. And then, when he looked around, he was struck by the fear in Lucy Cunningham's.

"How much longer is this going to take?" Frank demanded. "We were asked to be here at eleven and it's already half past."

"I cannot say, sir. Please be patient. They will be ready for you soon."

"Can't you ask them?"

"Please be patient. They will be ready for you soon," the officer repeated.

"You can't treat us like that!" Frank complained. "I know what you're trying to do, this is your one chance to be the big shots over the decent Christian people, right? What are you trying to do, sweat a confession out of us? It's not going to work, you know, because we've got nothing to hide!"

The doors behind the counter opened just then and Carla Saito emerged, Officer Pang showing her out.

"Harry Sullivan?" Officer Pang said.

"Why don't you two go in first," Harry suggested to the Cunninghams. "That's all right, isn't it? I don't mind waiting."

The walls of the Bukit Tinggi Neighbourhood Police Post were not soundproof.

Carla Saito did not have much to say and Senior Staff Sergeant Salim believed in giving people with nothing to say plenty of time not to say it. So they, along with Officer Pang, stationed by the dormant recording equipment, had been able to follow Frank Cunningham's speech in the waiting room very clearly. Indeed Officer Pang had made a move toward the door, meaning to ask them to quiet down, but the smallest gesture from SSS Salim stopped him. He saw it was not just the conversation that interested Salim but the effect Frank Cunningham's loudly expressed opinions were having on Carla Saito. Officer Pang was a quick learner. He settled back to watch Carla Saito too. The woman was not only withholding information from them, as SSS Salim clearly suspected . . . she was also a very angry woman.

"You want to go out there to talk to that man?" SSS Salim asked, suddenly and casually. "You look like you got a lot of things to say to him."

"Oh, I have things to say to him all right!" burst out Carla Saito. "But someone like him wouldn't want to hear anything I say!"

"But I do," SSS Salim said agreeably. "Say what you want to say. Then I can put it down and say we've done the interview."

Carla Saito hesitated, still suspicious.

"You can look over your statement," SSS Salim offered. "Read it over before you sign it. If you don't like it, don't sign."

"It's no big deal," Carla Saito said. "I never met Laura Kwee, so I can't say anything about how she dressed. But no man has a right to say it's how women dress that gets them attacked by men. If men feel so excited by women wearing short skirts or so threatened by them wearing pants, then they're the ones that have a problem!"

"I agree," said SSS Salim.

"Is there anything else?"

"You didn't see anyone else loitering outside the café before you went in?"

"I didn't say I was loitering there. But okay, I was outside for a while, deciding whether to go in. Laura Kwee had been sending Marianne messages about the wine dining events and I thought she would be there. I thought I could have a quick word with her before she went in, that's all. But I didn't see her."

"Did you see anybody else? Using a phone maybe?"

Harry Sullivan stopped Carla Saito before she got to the door. "We met—briefly—the other night at the café. Don't suppose you remember. You were a bit upset. You came looking for Laura Kwee."

"What do you want?"

"I was just wondering if you're all right. I mean, we all got thrown into this. Turn up for a dinner and a bit of a drink and end up in a police station. I'm not saying it's never happened to me before, but I didn't expect it to be happening here! Did they tell you not to leave the country? Have you got someplace to stay?"

Carla managed a laugh. "I suppose I'm as free to go as I could be. They haven't told me I can't leave the country."

"How has your stay in Singapore been, otherwise?"

She looked at him curiously. "If you were there that

night, you'll have gathered this isn't exactly a tourist holiday for me."

When it was finally his turn, Harry Sullivan told SSS Salim
he had come to Singapore in search of work. "I found I
couldn't settle down to retirement. I had enough to live
on, but that's not everything, is it?"

SSS Salim had not even gotten to his questions about
Laura Kwee and her phone, and here the man was already
nervous. Not that either Salim or Officer Pang seemed to
notice this. Foreigners were often apprehensive on first
encounter with the Singapore police; some might have
had unpleasant encounters with the authorities in their
own countries, and others—like Mr. Sullivan, SSS Salim
thought—probably believed police-state propaganda.

Officer Pang was painstakingly listing details of Harry
Sullivan's passport (already photocopied) on a form, and
as SSS Salim waited for him to finish he asked: "So, how do
you like Singapore so far?"

"Fine. It's good. Of course, it may not be my thing, but
I'll give it a fair chance."

"And your line is?"

"I was in the import-export business. And dealing with
oil products. So I have all the contacts, you see."

"Sorry you got mixed up in this business. We just have a
few question and then—"

"Officer, I know I'm here to talk about the message supposedly sent from the dead girl's phone. But there's some-

thing I think you should know. The background. What happened at the previous dinner. That's when I first met them. Laura Kwee and the other girl that's supposed to be missing—you'll have heard all about it if you were talking to her friend that just came out. Have you found her yet, by the way?"

"Marianne Peters? Not yet."

"Pity. I really liked Marianne. I had hoped to get to know her better, in fact. That was the first time we met. We talked about having a drink together sometime, but that night she said she had to meet someone . . ." Harry sensed both officers become more alert at this. The officer with the notepad stopped writing and the one sitting opposite Harry Sullivan checked that the recorder on the table was on and edged it closer to him.

"Did Marianne Peters mention who she was going to meet?"

"I don't think so. No, she didn't. But I got the impression it was someone special." He lowered his voice. "But better not mention it to that young woman who just left. I got the impression there's something going on between them. Or so one would like to think, anyway."

This was noted, though the senior officer did not remark on it. "Marianne Peters didn't give you any idea who she was meeting? Male or female . . . family member perhaps?"

The way he had picked on that point for further questioning made Harry Sullivan certain that the police knew something had happened to Marianne. "Do you mean she's really missing? I thought it was just that woman over-reacting. If you asked me, I would have said Marianne probably chose to duck out of the way because that woman was being a stalker." Again he triggered a spike in interest. And again they said nothing.

"That first week was so long ago. I think Laura went back in to talk to Selina. She was pretty upset about what happened, I remember. We all were a bit. I thought it was a big joke, but you know how people are here."

"What happened?" the officer asked. Of course he knew, Harry Sullivan thought, he just wanted to hear another side of the story. Well, since he was there, he would give them all the help he could.

"Laura Kwee had some trouble holding her liquor. She wasn't used to it. She was drinking and talking loudly, you know how they are. The ones that aren't used to it are the worst. She had made cupcakes. She was going on about decorating them, how she planned to make her own engagement and wedding cakes herself out of cupcakes because decorating them was an art form. Gave me the impression she had a bit of a crush on our chief instructor, if you ask me. His wife saw it too. I think she was more put out than he was.

"Selina, is that right? Mrs. Selina Lee. She was still in there with the drunk woman and Marianne went back in there to talk to them. Her brother and his wife had al-ready gone off. I got the impression Marianne wanted to smooth things over before anything got too out of hand.

She was that kind of girl, very peace loving. A peacemaker. Selina was going to call a taxi to get Laura home and Marianne said she could share it with her, but Selina said that was ridiculous because Marianne lived five minutes away. But that was the kind of thing Marianne would offer to do. She was a really nice girl. Not that anything serious could have worked out between us, of course. I'm happy being on my own right now. No sense rushing into anything, right? Much better to settle down, see where I am and where I'm going first."

SSS Salim thought the man was protesting too much. He guessed Harry Sullivan had asked Marianne Peters out and been turned down.

"The woman who got drunk—that was Laura Kwee, wasn't it?"

Harry Sullivan nodded. "I didn't like to say—with how things ended up and all. But she was pretty much plastered."

"And you thought that she might be having an affair with someone there? Like Mark Lee?"

Harry shook his head. "I think she had a thing for him. And from the way he was reacting, I'd say he'd done her a couple of times. But affair—no way. I know people, you know what I mean? I sense things that are going on. I think Laura Kwee had something on with her friend's husband and he was trying to dump her. It was all the tension there. That night she was all over him, saying it was stupid to hide his feelings from her when everybody already knew and so on. How she loved baking and his wife wouldn't even fry him an egg. It was clear his wifey didn't like it. I don't know if she was aware the two of them were carrying on before, but after that she sure did. We all did. If I were you, I would look into that. You should go and find out more about her."

SSS Salim made a mental note to ask Mark Lee and his wife about this. He had already spoken to both of them earlier, but neither had mentioned it—not surprising, perhaps. Officer Pang made a note. Attempts to meet them again had been fended off with the excuse that they were both very busy all the time. But that was how it was with most people in Singapore unless they were tourists or retired. SSS Salim was all for respecting the residents, but if Mark and Selina Lee did not make time to see him soon, he was going to have to insist.

"So do you have any thoughts on what might have happened that night after Laura left? Or who may have sent that text if not her?"

Harry Sullivan paused before speaking. He had not expected the police to ask his opinion, though he should have. After all, he had been present when the message came through.

"It might have been a complete stranger—to the dinners, I mean. Obviously it had to be someone Laura Kwee knew. Maybe he or she wanted to see whether Laura would be missed and wanted to delay the alarm being raised till he could leave the country or something like that."

SSS Salim seemed to think that this was a good point. "But wouldn't it be more important for the person who sent the message to make sure her colleagues at work, her family, and so on didn't miss her?"

"Maybe he did. Maybe he's just a very thorough person, who believes in covering all bases."

That was true too. But though SSS Salim did not say so, thoroughness was not a term he would have chosen to describe whoever had put Laura Kwee into the sea.

"You were outside for some time smoking, I hear—"

"So? That's not a crime, is it?"

"Actually it is. But that's not the issue right now. Did you see anyone while you were there? Man, woman, anyone who seemed to be watching or hanging around?"

"No. And no offense, but I still have some trouble telling people apart here. Right now they all still look the same to me."

Neither Harry Sullivan nor the Cunninghams had added anything substantial to SSS Salim's information. All they could say was that Laura Kwee had definitely been expected until the arrival of her text message. And that Selina had been so angry that the anger could not have been put on.

Frank Cunningham had said, "There was something not quite right that night, but I can't put my finger on what it was. Part of the problem of growing old."

SSS Salim did not make much of that. People were

always sensing something strange after something strange had already happened. He did not really think any of the people he had spoken to that day had anything to do with Laura Kwee's death. All he was trying to do was establish where Laura Kwee had been last seen or heard from. A neighbor had seen her arriving home in a taxi the night of the previous wine dining. Thanks to this neighbor and the taxi company, they had managed to trace the driver of the taxi, who remembered Laura but could not remember her saying or doing anything that would be helpful to the investigation. The next morning Laura had phoned her office to say she was down with the flu and taking two days off. SSS Salim double-checked that the colleague Laura called had spoken to her in person.

"Yes, it was her for certain."

"No, she didn't sound funny or anything. I mean she sounded really sick. I told her to be sure to go to the doctor because she sounded really sick. Do you know what happened to her yet?"

So Laura had been alive then. "Did she call you from her home phone or her mobile phone, do you know?"

"Laura only had a mobile phone because she was the only one living there. She took her phone everywhere with her, so she didn't see any reason to pay for another line."

And Laura had taken her phone home with her. But then, if Laura had taken her phone home, how had it gotten into the burning bin outside Aunty Lee's Delights?

SSS Salim was still waiting to hear back from Laura's parents in Malaysia. They said they wouldn't be able to make it down to Singapore but would send a family representative and gave permission for the police to go through the things in Laura's flat. They didn't know anything about a boyfriend or problems or whether anyone had threatened Laura recently.

"She was a very good girl," her mother said on the phone. "She would phone us once a month. And every time she would tell us not to worry about her. We wanted her to settle down. Get married. We wanted to find her a good husband. But she enjoyed her independence too much. Especially after—" The gentle voice broke off.

"Especially after what?"

"I'm sorry. Nothing. We knew she was seeing some man."

Laura's father's voice cut in. "She never had any time to come back and see us. She used to phone once a month but lately we never heard from her. If her mother tried to phone her, she would get angry because she was so busy, had no time to talk. I knew that she must be seeing some man. So serious about him she had no time to talk to her own parents. What is the point of having children? I ask you. When they grow up they all have no time for their parents!"

Whether or not Laura Kwee had been involved with someone in Singapore, she had certainly lost touch with her family in Penang. That was the sad thing about chances that can lead to a better life, SSS Salim thought, remembering the scholarships that had opened doors for him. If you succeeded in creating a new life for yourself, what happened to the people who had been a part of the old one? On an impulse he picked up his cell phone and called his mother. As it rang he wondered whether he had time to make it back to her flat for dinner; she was sure to invite him.

"Call from Central on line one," Officer Song opened the door to say. "Sounds like bad news. And there's something strange about Miss Laura Kwee's apartment. It looks like somebody broke into it, but it must have happened after she disappeared, according to the neighbors."

SSS Salim cut off his own phone before it was answered. He knew what the bad news was before he heard it. In fact, ever since speaking to old Mrs. Lee, he had been expecting it. There was no way he would be making it home to see his mother that night.

In spite of a dampening weather prediction of "scattered showers over some parts of Singapore," it was crowded on Sentosa, the resort island off Singapore, over the Chinese New Year. This year the first day of the lunar new year fell on a Thursday. Many local people would be visiting relatives or Chinese friends and colleagues while those less socially or traditionally inclined took advantage of the nine-day holiday stretch that materialized if one judiciously applied for just three days of leave between weekends. Because of that, most of the people who had crossed over to Sentosa from Singapore that day via causeway, boardwalk, cable car, monorail, or ferry were tourists. For the most part they were looking for ways to occupy themselves since the Chinese New Year was the one time of year when Singaporeans focused more on themselves and families than on pleasing tourists and other visitors.

It was a visiting Canadian couple who got tired of crowds and giant rabbits, crafted out of plastic, plants, and soda cans for the incoming Chinese zodiac year, the Year of the Rabbit. They went off the beaten track. The husband was an amateur botanist interested in tropical flora and his wife was sufficiently in love with him not to find his passion tedious. Plunging muddily through the mangroves, they found themselves at last at the junction of waters where debris washed up by the incoming waves lurked till the tides changed their direction again.

"Look at all the garbage. All that plastic—think of the poor sea creatures. It's terrible."

"And the smell—there is a dead fish somewhere. Or maybe it's a dead dog . . . Look, over there—there's something in a bag—"

But it was not a dead dog. It was the body of a very dead woman.

9

Marianne Peters

Aunty Lee slept deeply but restlessly. She was sitting facing M. L. Lee and he was smiling as he said to her, "Can I take your hand?" And Aunty Lee felt so overwhelmingly happy, wanting to say so many things at the same time, from "Yes! Yes!" to "Do you remember those are the words that you proposed to me with? And every time you say them to me, I feel as though you are proposing to me again?" and "That is what I miss about you most of all—now I can look at you all the time but I can never touch you," and she was a young woman again; the young girl M. L. Lee had proposed to.

And then she saw Nina. For a moment she was angry with her. Nina of all people should have known how little time Aunty Lee had with her husband now that he was dead. Nina was approaching them, walking toward them from a great distance across the *padang* with a piece of paper—Aunty Lee knew at once that it was a telegram carrying bad news; apart from the one announcing the birth of a child, most telegrams brought news of death. Aunty Lee decided she and M. L. Lee would run away from Nina. She already knew what the bad news was, but as long as Nina did not deliver the telegram, it did not have to be true. But M. L. Lee did not run with her. He was already fading and insubstantial and Aunty Lee could not feel the hands she tried to take in her own desperate fingers. The knowledge she was trying so hard to deny was already more substantial around her than the man she so longed to keep alive by her side.

"Wouldn't you rather know the truth?" M. L. Lee asked her without speaking.

"No. I don't want to know it. I don't want it to be true!" Aunty Lee thought desperately at him.

"That *ang moh* man asks very funny questions," M. L. Lee said to her. "You should see what he has written about you so far in his notebook. He is writing about you for that magazine, you know."

Aunty Lee said desperately, "I don't care what anybody writes as long as you stay alive." But it was no good. She had lost him again. The downside of hope was how rapidly and miserably you crashed each time you lost it. Again.

Then Aunty Lee realized that Nina was not telling her

that M. L. Lee was dead. They had moved back into the present (she knew, as she noticed the liver-colored age spots on her hands) and Nina was saying, "They found another body. They think it is Marianne Peters," and Aunty Lee looked around to see that she was not the only one who did not want to hear the news. Carla Saito was sitting curled up on the ground, scrunched up into a ball with her hands covering her ears to shut out the news. Beyond her, standing close together, Aunty Lee could see Marianne Peters's family: her father and mother, her brother and his wife, and, next to them, Mathilda, M. L. Lee's daughter, who was saying, "Aren't you glad I'm safely far away in England?"

"Should we tell her?" Nina said, now standing over Carla Saito. "You should tell her. Her friend is dead. She will want to know."

No, she wouldn't, Aunty Lee thought. She would certainly not want to hear. But Nina was going to tell Carla and Aunty Lee knew she had to stop her. This was not news you could just break to someone. Aunty Lee knew this because she knew what it was like to be given "news" you already knew but were doing all you could to shut out. But Nina and Carla Saito were suddenly miles away, though Aunty Lee could still see them clearly, the way one can see only in dreams, and even as Aunty Lee struggled to shout out to Nina, she could tell it was too late.

And then Aunty Lee woke up. It was still dark in her bedroom. Her morning tea was not yet on her bedside table. That meant it was not yet six-thirty in the morning and that M. L. Lee was long dead. Aunty Lee lay savoring her regret for a moment, then she remembered the events of the previous evening and she was instantly wide-awake.

Aunty Lee pressed the buzzer for Nina. It was just past six but Nina appeared within minutes with her tea and the newspapers. Aunty Lee fumbled through the books and papers on her bedside table looking for her reading glasses.

"Did Salim find out anything else?" Aunty Lee asked Nina. "Anything that's not in the papers?" Not finding her spectacles, she reached for the newspapers anyway.

"Drink your tea, ma'am," Nina said. Deftly she stacked the things on the bedside table, retrieved the reading glasses from behind the table lamp, and handed them to her employer.

Something in Nina's manner made Aunty Lee stop fussing to watch her. "Tell me," she said.

"Ma'am, they found the dead body of Marianne Peters."

"Identified?"

"Yes, ma'am."

Without saying anything further, Aunty Lee put on her spectacles and read the article for herself. SECOND MURDER VICTIM FOUND ON SENTOSA, the headline screamed. After saying the body had been identified as that of Marianne Beatrice Peters, aged twenty-eight, it went on to say that this second female body was less decomposed than Laura Kwee's had been. Though this body was similarly packed in plastic wrap, it seemed to have been more meticulously wrapped and taped, which might have been why it had taken longer for enough decomposition gases to bloat it up enough to bring it to the surface. Preliminary tests suggested that this victim probably died several days before Laura Kwee, who had been found on Sunday morning.

"Ma'am, you want me to bring your soft egg and toast up here?" Nina was also shocked by the news, but feeding her employer was her responsibility.

"No. I'll get up and go downstairs. We're going out and I want to prepare some things first." Aunty Lee swung her legs off the bed, startling Nina. She had her own responsibilities as she saw them.

"Are we going to see Professor and Mrs. Peters, ma'am?"

"No. I want to drop off a note, thank you for reminding me, but I think they will have enough on their minds right now—"

SSS Salim studied the report. Two bodies of young women found in four days—this was something that belonged on television, not on the beaches of law-abiding Singapore. Press and public opinion would be all over them for not doing anything to catch the killer before he struck again.

It was not that Salim was afraid of being blamed—he was a very small fish in this pond. What surprised him was that this information had been sent to him at all. It was true that one of the dead women had lived in his jurisdiction, but because of the family concerned, he had not even had to take on the task of notifying them. It turned out that the commissioner of police was a family friend of the Peterses' and was taking care of it personally. Salim had no doubt that everything would be taken care of by senior, experienced officers.

He was not sorry about this. SSS Salim knew he was a responsible, hardworking man who had risen through the ranks through his own efforts. He could do a good routine job. But when it came to crimes like this, he felt unskilled compared to officers with more qualifications—for example Commissioner Raja, who not only had a law degree from a Singapore university but further degrees in criminology and criminal psychology from Cambridge and Harvard . . . and who had already left two messages asking SSS Salim to call him in his office and then on his private cell phone when Salim arrived at work at 7:15 a.m.

SSS Salim's first thought was that he was being considered for transfer. This was swiftly discarded. He had only recently received his current appointment and had done nothing so far to justify further recognition. His second thought was that he was being reprimanded. One dead woman had been last seen alive in his neighborhood jurisdiction and the other had lived there. Or HQ had found someone more senior and experienced to put in charge of this suddenly hot district. A transfer would be unfair and unjust, but Salim felt it not unlikely. He also realized that he did not want to give up his posting even though he had not wanted it to begin with. But he could hardly tell his superiors that he wanted to stay on because the recent deaths had suddenly made the job interesting.

He put the call through to the commissioner, feeling a mixture of dread and determination. But what the police commissioner said took him completely by surprise. Even now he was not sure what to do about it. He had not mentioned it to the rest of the staff, who were no doubt also wondering whether he was being fired or demoted. He had not joined them in placing breakfast "orders," but they had brought him a packet of Kopi-O (black coffee with sugar) and a packet of noodles nonetheless. He had not paid anyone for them and both remained untouched on the side table in his office when he heard the knock on his door.

"Sir?" Officer Pang opened the door without waiting to be invited in. The younger man had spent as little time asleep as Salim had, but seemed very little the worse for wear. Salim suddenly felt old. He was in his thirties, his mother was always reminding him no woman would marry a policeman (high danger, low pay), and now the hours were starting to get him down. Perhaps it was time to start looking around for another line of work. But what? When Officer Pang did not continue, SSS Salim looked up from his papers to see what was wrong.

Aunty Lee was standing right behind Officer Pang. The only reason she was still outside his office was that Officer Pang had physically blocked the doorway with his uniformed bulk—for the time being at least. Even though the top of Aunty Lee's head barely reached above the officer's shoulder, she was already making inroads into the office, looking around him and even under his arm.

"Senior Staff Sergeant Salim? Can we just have a moment of your time?"

"Madam, please," Officer Pang told her patiently, "will you wait outside. I will inform you if he is free to see you—"

"It's still so early. I'm sure you haven't had time for breakfast. You are allowed to eat here, right? You have to keep your strength up on the job."

SSS Salim gestured to his assistant to let his visitors in. He might as well make one old lady happy that morning. Of course he had work waiting for him, but then he always had work waiting, that was nothing new.

Aunty Lee had brought him breakfast. Nina followed him through the door that Officer Pang held open, looking both amused and confused. Terrorists should dress up as old ladies, SSS Salim reflected. Regardless of their training, most Singapore officers were conditioned to show respect to their elders, however eccentric. He gave Officer Pang an excusing nod.

"Yes, Mrs. Lee? How can I help you?"

"Hello, Salim. Actually I was hoping we could help each other. Such terrible news, right? That poor, poor girl. I watched her grow up, you know. And it must be so terrible for her parents also. Such a shock. They thought she was on holiday, you know?"

It so happened that SSS Salim did know this. He was pleased to be able to say, "We have already spoken to them. Of course, we welcome any information that you can give us, but you know you can always make a report even if you don't see me—"

Aunty Lee had settled herself down in one of the two chairs facing him. Nina laid out the breakfast they had brought for him: homemade *nasi lemak*, a coconut-cream-coated rice dish that was already fragrant through the waxy banana leaf that enclosed it. Nina unwrapped the steaming package to reveal fried egg, deep-fried *ikan kuning*, cucumber slices, and a generous dollop of sambal over a mix of *ikan bilis* and peanuts.

"Don't worry," Aunty Lee said. "We also brought for your people outside. Also some *epok-epok* for later. My special recipe—we made both sardine and potato."

"This could be considered bribery." SSS Salim was only partly joking.

"Nonsense. We citizens want to show our appreciation to you nice young men for keeping us safe . . . what's so wrong with that? Anyway, you have to eat, right? If this is your breakfast time, then I am not taking up so much of your work time. Anyway, I spoke to your Commissioner Raja—"

"What?" Startled, SSS Salim half stood up in his seat.

"Careful you don't spill your tea. I made masala tea. It is a new recipe, I'm still experimenting. You tell me what you think of it? Where was I? Oh yes. I met your commissioner, that nice Inspector Raja, at the Peterses' place yesterday. I told him I had spoken with you about this—even before the poor girl was found."

SSS Salim wondered whether Aunty Lee had just managed to sabotage his whole career.

"I told him when we spoke you were concerned about poor Marianne and tried to investigate her whereabouts, but her family insisted she was away on holiday. And I thought that if given the opportunity, you could probably pick up a lot more because you are here at grassroots level."

"I see," SSS Salim said, though he did not see. He suspected that the commissioner had been caught by surprise by Aunty Lee and mouthed polite responses till someone came to rescue him.

"So I told him what I thought he should do and he said I could speak to you, to see if you are okay with it."

"I see," SSS Salim said again. The *nasi lemak* smelled temptingly of coconut, reminding him of how his late grandmother's *nasi lemak* used to taste. Recently he had only tasted the dish out of the takeaway packets sold along the walk from the MRT station. He could have afforded a car, but reasoned that he had the official car for official duties, and if the minister for transport could take the train to work, he felt he ought to too. Besides, there was always the matter of saving up for the future . . .

Looking across to Nina, Salim saw she was watching him as though following his thoughts, and he quickly looked away. He was being absurd.

"So what do you have to tell me?" he asked Aunty Lee.

"I got these for you." Aunty Lee put a file on the table. "The contacts for the friends that Marianne Peters was supposed to be on holiday with. And what they said she told them. It's all there. I think they were afraid of being blamed by the family or accused of lying by the police, so they didn't say much at your official interview, but I think you'll find it quite interesting. There was definitely someone else involved. You'll see, they say she mentioned someone trying to lend her his chalet to show what a nice guy he is? And after this, I'm going to talk to Carla Saito—you've already interviewed her, right?—about exactly what Marianne was hoping to do. Why don't you try your *epok-epok* before it gets cold? I made it this morning. Straight from the kitchen. Your commissioner likes it very much also. By the way, he thinks very highly of you, you know."

Salim took a tentative bite of the fried batter puff. If it was good enough for Commissioner Raja, it was good enough for him. Then he forgot all about the commissioner as the hot savory mix of chili, onion, sardine, and—was it lime?—burst out of its crisp casing in his mouth. This was possibly the most sensational *epok-epok* he had tasted since his late grandmother's death. Unlike the usual Chinese version, the pastry was thick and rich, and the savory mix of seasoned fish, potato, and hard-boiled egg inside almost made him swoon. He looked across at Aunty Lee with something like devotion in his eyes.

"And I was wondering whether you had time to look at the Sentosa Landmark Villas yet."

"Beg your pardon?"

"If you take a look at this chart and follow the current patterns, doesn't it look as though a body found here"—a short but very red fingernail jabbed at the map—"would most likely have come from somewhere around here . . . especially if it was put into the water at high tide?"

SSS Salim had a feeling that Aunty Lee was reminding him of something he should have known. "My grandfather used to take me fishing around there," he said. "I should have thought of that. It's actually very true—very good. If anything comes of it, I will make sure to give you the credit . . ."

"Don't be silly, boy," Aunty Lee said fondly. "You just go and find out what you can."

"I still don't understand . . ." SSS Salim could not think of a way to finish his question without sounding rude. "I mean Commissioner Raja . . . he has never . . . I only met him once before this, when he attended our graduation . . . I don't think he even remembered me. How come—"

"He and I had met before," Aunty Lee said lightly. "Long ago, when there were fewer people in Singapore, everybody knew everybody else. Now, when people in our age group are starting to die out, those of us left are in the same situation. And we know who we can trust. So when the commissioner and I met again by chance at a friend's home, we both agreed that you are a nice, responsible young man. Of course he remembers you!"

"But why?" SSS Salim had to ask. Why did an upper-middle-class Tai-Tai worry about such sordid things? "Why are you so interested?"

"Because the two girls who died both came to eat in my restaurant. For me that makes it personal. If they ate my cooking, they are my guests and they are my family. Why don't you eat your *nasi lemak*? You don't like it, is it?"

Salim ate his *nasi lemak*.

Aunty Lee's next stop was Carla Saito's small room in the Frangipani Inn on Pasir Panjang Road. It was not a place Aunty Lee was familiar with and she took it all in with interest.

The Frangipani Inn could have been a stack of shoebox apartments except for the check-in counter that stood in the overdecorated foyer. There were plastic flowers everywhere. Though two girls, recent arrivals from the People's Republic of China by their accents, were wiping down the front window side by side as they talked. Nina noted there were smudges on the walls and dust on the corner of the counter where Aunty Lee put down her bag.

"Hourly rate or daily rate?" the concierge asked in a Filipino accent without looking up from his paper.

Aunty Lee waited. When the man finally looked at them, she said, "We are looking for Miss Carla Saito."

"Is she . . . is this person here with a man? Are you look-

ing for your husband? We cannot give out such information. It is all confidential. Hotel policy."

"I am looking for Carla Saito," Aunty Lee said sweetly.
"Of course, the room may be booked under the name
Marianne Peters."

"This is an interesting area."

The front desk finally agreed to call Carla Saito. Between her refusing to come down to the lobby and Aunty
Lee refusing to leave it, the beleaguered concierge eventu-
ally gave them her room number.

"It's not bad," Carla was saying. "There's a twenty-four-
hour prata place, a Chinese food place, a 7-Eleven, and a
laundry all in the next block. Which is useful, given there's
no café and no room service in the hotel. And that Ying-
Yang place looks like some kind of motorcycle rental. Nice
guy runs it. He feeds the stray cats. If we ended up staying,
I thought I might get a bike for transport.

"Marianne chose this place because she knew it from
her university days. She told me about the twenty-four-
hour cheese prata." Suddenly she fell silent. "I don't know
why I'm talking like this. What do you want?"

Aunty Lee knew how the young woman felt. What had
happened was not yet real to her. But somewhere inside,
she must have known for some time. And she was no
doubt feeling that nothing mattered anymore and would
never matter again. In the days following her husband's
death, Aunty Lee would have killed herself if there hadn't

been visitors constantly around her needing to be fed and looked after.

"Tell me," Aunty Lee said. She motioned to Nina to put the *tingkat* of hot soup on the small coffee table. Nina could not help wrinkling her nose at the griminess of the room and the thought of cheese prata. Nina liked cheese and she liked pratas—fried flatbreads usually served with mutton or vegetable curry—but she could not stomach the idea of a cheese prata combination made at the twenty-four-hour-stall around the corner on Clementi Road. She had never tried it, but to Nina things as different as Western cheese and Indian prata should not be combined.

Though unwashed and probably suffering from insomnia, Nina thought, but without the black-rimmed eyes she'd had the last time she and Aunty Lee had seen her, Carla Saito looked much younger and almost pretty.

"No, I don't want to talk to you," she suddenly declared. She stood up and marched toward them. "I don't want to have anything to do with you!"

Nina had not realized till now how tall Carla was. Instinctively she took a step backward, pulling on Aunty Lee's arm to make her move too, but Aunty Lee simply swung both her arm and Nina behind her, staying put.

"You're enjoying this, aren't you?" Carla Saito's voice was low and harsh from tears and dehydration. "You're just an old busybody and you've got nothing better to do, so you're meddling here. Get out of my room or I'm going to smash your stupid soup into your face!"

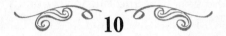

10

Carla Saito and Marianne Peters

"All right," said Aunty Lee. She blinked at Carla Saito, somehow not seeming to notice Nina's frantic tugging at her arm. "You can throw the soup at me if it makes you feel better. But doing that probably won't do you as much good as eating it."

Carla made an unconvincing sweeping gesture that encompassed Aunty Lee and the *tingkat* of hot soup that Nina had put on the table. Nina winced but Aunty Lee watched unperturbed. Carla's face suddenly began to twist in silent agony. She crumpled where she stood. As Nina thought later, it was as though all the bones in her body had just melted.

Instantly Aunty Lee was squatting with her arms around

the choking, shaking girl. "I know," she said. "I know, I know." When finally Carla started to cry in earnest, her moaning and muffled screams came as a relief after the tension that had blocked them. Nina found that she herself was shaking as well and sat down quietly on the only chair in the room. Neither Aunty Lee nor Carla, who continued holding on to her, seemed to notice.

"Both Laura and Marianne used to come to eat my food," Aunty Lee said. "I feel responsible for the people I feed. Once my food has gone into them and become part of them and their lives, I become part of their lives. In a way I love them. And I watched Marianne grow up, you know. And having lost someone who was very, very much the center of my life, I do know something of what you are going through.

"Besides," she continued, "you are hungry. You say it's not my business, but all hungry people are my business."

Now that she was somewhat calmer, Carla drank the soup. It was good soup, with very thinly sliced carrots, cherry tomatoes, baby corn, and mini bitter gourds in a clear dried shiitake and miso broth, with fragments of *kway teow* by then so impregnated with liquid flavor they could be swallowed without chewing.

Aunty Lee was right, Carla Saito thought. Solving the most immediate of her hungers gave her strength to attack the others.

"Thank you," she said to the grave old woman who

had watched her eat. "I needed that. What are we going to do now?"

"Tell me about Marianne," Aunty Lee said. "Tell me what you are keeping secret and what you think her parents still don't know."

Carla had already given her statement to the police, who had not arrested or accused her of anything. But they had advised her not to leave Singapore just yet. They had not said how long their "not just yet" might last. She seemed strangely unperturbed by this injunction. In her position, Nina was certain she would have been climbing up the walls. But then she had never been in Carla Saito's position. Aunty Lee seemed to understand. She waited.

"Anyway, I have nowhere else to go," Carla said in the same emotionless monotone in which she had answered all Aunty Lee's questions. That served to explain both why she had no objection to remaining in Singapore and, perhaps, why she was willing to talk to Aunty Lee after her initial show of resistance.

"Marianne told me that the real reason she went to Washington was to commit suicide." She looked hard at Aunty Lee, searching for a reaction. Aunty Lee opened her eyes and looked satisfactorily startled.

"Why would she do such a thing?"

"Because she didn't want to upset her family, her parents. But she felt she just couldn't go on living here the way they expected her to. She could not live with what she had become in their eyes. She thought that if she died over there, they would put it down to depression or even think it was an accident or something . . . Anyway, they wouldn't blame themselves for it. I thought I had stopped her from considering such thoughts. I thought I saved her when we met. I thought it was like magic, that that's what brought us together."

Carla Saito paused, then added, "That's the real reason she was in Washington. She didn't want to kill herself in Singapore because of her family. In spite of everything, she cared very much for her family."

"You didn't tell the police that?"

"It wasn't relevant."

"Surely it would be just as bad for her family wherever she killed herself," Aunty Lee pointed out gently.

"But it would not be something they would have to re-member every time they had to look at or pass by the place where it happened. And she said that if she died so far away, they could believe it was an accident or something if they wanted to."

Aunty Lee reflected that whatever Marianne's reasons for wanting to kill herself, she had not wanted to hurt her family.

In spite of the shock of learning of Marianne Peters's death, Carla Saito now seemed more in control of herself than she'd been on her previous visits to Aunty Lee's De-lights. At least knowing that the worst had happened took away the raging uncertainty. Aunty Lee knew from her own experience, however, that the physical reality of death had not yet sunk in. In Carla's case, it would take even longer than it usually did because so much of her relationship with Marianne had been spent apart from each other. Even if Carla's mind knew that Marianne Peters was dead, her heart would continue waiting for the next phone call, the next blip on the computer screen that announced that her friend was online and waiting to hear from her. It was like being suspended in purgatory with occasional glimpses into hell.

"Do you need to tell anybody what happened?" Aunty Lee asked. "Won't anybody back home be wondering where you are?"

"There's no one to worry. I quit my job and sold my place. I wanted to tie up all my loose ends, in case I ended up never going back. I suppose I will, though, sooner or later. Meanwhile I haven't done anything about getting a ticket yet."

Aunty Lee filled Carla's cup of tea from the thermos. It was chrysanthemum tea, said to be calming; Carla Saito might be speaking slowly, but the way her eyes moved constantly over the table and around the room even as she spoke suggested there was a lot of tension beneath the surface. Right now it was blanketed by grief and exhaustion, but Aunty Lee was not going to feed it in any way if she could help it.

"You were telling me about meeting Marianne in Washington. You said you didn't want to say anything earlier in case it got her into trouble with her parents?"

Carla looked at Aunty Lee. "She spent a lot of time in your café, didn't she? She said she liked it there, that it was like her second home. And she liked you."

"I hope so. I think she did. Otherwise she wouldn't have come." Aunty Lee smiled. "Marianne didn't do what she didn't want to do." She could tell Carla was not ignoring her query so much as working herself around to a starting point.

Carla shook her head slightly but seemed to agree. "You knew her family, right? You knew her when she was growing up?"

"Not really. By the time I married my late husband, she and her brother were already almost teenagers. I think she was eleven or twelve. Her parents were friends of my late husband and his wife. Mark would remember her better. You met my stepson, Mark, at the café that night, didn't you?"

Carla Saito remembered and dismissed the subject. "I wish I'd told her to forget her family, let them think she was dead, and just stay with me in Washington."

"Should her family blame themselves?"

"Because she's dead now? Of course not. Marianne didn't kill herself. How can you even think that? Didn't you read about how she was found? Wrapped in plastic bags?"

Aunty Lee fluttered her hands apologetically. "No, no, no. That is not what I meant. Forgive me, I am an old lady and sometimes I don't put things very well. I mean, were they responsible for how Marianne was feeling when you first met her in Washington?"

"No. Or maybe yes. I mean, they were responsible in that they created the environment and everything. Marianne said it wasn't their fault. She said traditional Indian families in Asia are always overprotective, especially of their daughters."

Aunty Lee would have thought that traditional families everywhere in the world were protective of their daughters.

"I know I talked her out of killing herself that time. I told Marianne if she was going to die anyway, why not just run away, disappear, and start over? Just as bad for her family as if she killed herself, true, but not as bad for her. She would have a new start and they would feel better about it in time. I did not tell you that earlier because I wondered or hoped that something had happened to make Marianne freak out and run off just to get away from them. Her family had that effect on her. So I wanted to speak to family members or someone who knew the family—Laura Kwee and you in this case—to help me find out whether anything had happened in the Peters family just before Marianne vanished."

"Laura Kwee?" Aunty Lee asked.

"That's why I was looking for her. She told Mari that someone offered us the use of his holiday chalet on Sentosa. Because he'd booked it for a special two-week stay, but his friend had to cancel. He knew she was a lesbian because Laura had found out and told him. Mari was so mad at Laura, so this was like a peace offering. He said she could go look at the place and then decide. But she pretty much decided right away because she said it couldn't be any worse than this place"—Carla waved her hand to encompass the room—"plus it was free and much bigger, and being in a chalet on Sentosa meant that we wouldn't be holed up in a room all the time in case someone saw her and told her parents she was in Singapore. But after that, I never heard from her again. And she never canceled the reservation, so I came here to wait for her."

"Marianne said it was a man who offered her the chalet on Sentosa? Are you sure she didn't mention a name?"

"I don't think she said it was a guy, but from the way she talked about it, that's the impression I got. Oh, it was a guy all right. Mari said she thought Laura would have liked her to turn down the offer so she could go to Sentosa with him herself, but she was still angry with Laura, so she was going to accept. She said I shouldn't be so suspicious of people."

"Suspicious? Were you?"

Carla Saito rubbed her already red eyes. Without makeup, the shadows beneath them were dark enough to look like bruises. "Not any more suspicious than I was of anyone else. That's the worst of it, right? I was always warning Marianne to be careful, she never believed me when I told her people were interested in her. And then, when this perverted bastard came along, I didn't sense a thing. I just let her walk right into it."

"Stop being so self-centered," Aunty Lee said.

Carla looked taken aback. "What?"

"This is not about you. It is about whoever persuaded Marianne to go to Sentosa with him. He is the one we should be thinking about. You can spend the rest of your life wondering whether or not you should have been more suspicious, but is that going to find the man who might have killed her?"

"You really think there's any chance we can find who did this to her?"

Aunty Lee looked at Carla. For once, she saw no cynicism or sarcasm in her features, only a forlorn person hungering for hope. Aunty Lee desperately wanted to feed that hope, but she was always wary of making promises to demons and she was not yet certain this tense young woman was not harboring a demon within her.

"I don't know whether there is a chance," Aunty Lee said honestly. "You are still young and strong. You can go away and move on with your life, but an old lady like me, I know that I cannot go on with my life without trying to find out the truth."

Whether she was a demon or not, the answer worked for Carla Saito.

"I want to find out too."

"Then tell me everything that Marianne Peters said to you about this person. And anything else she mentioned over the last few months. I want you to tell me everything you remember, down to the smallest detail."

In life as in recipes, it was often the smallest pinch of contrasting flavor—the lightest splash of seasoning savored undetected—that made all the difference to a dish.

Carla Saito pressed a few keys on her phone then handed it to Aunty Lee, who waved it away without trying to read the text message.

"Better you read it to me. By the time I find my spectacles, I have forgotten what I wanted to read."

" 'Don't have details yet but may have much better place for us to stay.' I called her back right away, of course, but she said she couldn't talk. She was with people. She said she would call back but she didn't."

"Why didn't you tell the police all this?"

"I knew the police were going to suspect me. They were already asking why I came to Singapore because nobody believes I would fly out here just to see Marianne. If I told them about us, I was afraid they would just blame everything on me and stop looking for the real culprit."

Aunty Lee thought about this. "They'll do their job."

"How can you say that?"

"This is Singapore. Most of our murders here come from domestic disputes and nightclub fights. They will suspect you first because you and Marianne were having a relationship. If you are innocent, they will move on to the next suspect. That is how it works here. By the book and step-by-step." And of course they sometimes got help from concerned citizens, but Aunty Lee did not mention this.

Even in school there were always extra tutors and exam aids to help students ace important tests.

"Do you think her family will mind if I go to the funeral?" Carla asked.

Aunty Lee did not know. She did not even know whether there was going to be a funeral at all. What was the correct procedure for burying a murder victim?

"I will talk to them. But there's no reason why you should not be there. You can come with me."

"Marianne and I did quarrel, you know. Before I came out. That's why I thought maybe . . ."

"Maybe she changed her mind."

Carla Saito nodded. "It was stupid. I thought she was being too idealistic. Like all the freedom-to-marry, vegan, freegan stuff. I lived in all that. I knew she was just struck by how new it was to her to be involved in a relationship with another woman and feared that it wouldn't last. I wanted us to be comfortable together. But as it turned out, it lasted for her all the rest of her life, didn't it?"

"You triggered the search," Aunty Lee said to Carla Saito. "That made all the difference."

"No, it didn't," Carla said bitterly. "At least to Marianne it makes no difference at all."

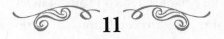

11

Meal Planning

"Ma'am. It is wrong."

"What are you talking about, Nina?"

"She said the way they love each other, like husband and wife . . . That is wrong—right?" Nina said.

The problem with people, Aunty Lee thought, was that you never knew what was going to surface when you stirred a stick in the mud. Of course, some people thought the best solution was to leave aside the stick and enjoy a calm surface. Most of the time Aunty Lee agreed with this. Even the best stock left some questionable debris settled at the bottom of the pot. But then even the best stockpots needed a thorough scrubbing out regularly. The key, of course, was knowing when to let settle and when to scrub.

"What is wrong to you may not be wrong to them," Aunty Lee pointed out.

"But if everybody thinks like them, then there will be no more babies, then what will happen?"

"I didn't have babies. Do you think I'm wrong too?"

This was not the answer Nina had expected. But this issue was too grounded in her core beliefs to be surrendered so easily.

"Ma'am, that is different. You got married. So if it is God's will, He will send you babies to bless you. People like them, they don't even want to get married. That is wrong."

Aunty Lee thought Carla Saito and Marianne Peters would very likely have married—and had a happy marriage—if they could have done so. Things were changing. They just had not changed fast enough for Marianne Peters. That, however, was not the issue inside Nina's head. But what went on between Marianne and Carla was no more Nina's business than Nina's beliefs were Aunty Lee's. She had heard Nina's attitude before, though expressed by other people and directed at other targets. The "desperate decency of the respectable poor" held true at all levels.

"We are going to close the shop for a while. One week, at least. I want you to e-mail all the people on the mailing list and tell them. And phone everybody who left orders with us. Tell them we're very sorry, but we're going to be closed for—better say two weeks."

"Ma'am! We cannot do that!" Nina forgot her philosophical problems with lesbians, given this practical dilemma. "Don't close the shop! What will people say? If you don't feel well, then I will prepare for them the orders—and I will look after you, of course, ma'am. But you cannot close the shop!" To Nina, who had been helping Aunty Lee since the establishment of Aunty Lee's Delights and who knew how quickly a business could fail, this was madness.

"Nonsense. Nobody is going to starve to death if we close the shop for a few days. And we're going to be very busy. First we are going to make two big yam cakes for the Peterses. Even if they don't feel like it, they should eat, and they are going to be getting visitors over. And tell them that if they let us know when they are arranging the wake and service for Marianne, we will provide all the food. At such a time they shouldn't have to think about food, but people still have got to eat.

"Then," she continued, "we are going to get in touch with the people from the last wine dining and tell them that since they cannot leave Singapore yet, they can come to our place to eat . . . say between eleven a.m. and three p.m. every day. Then they can come for a late breakfast and lunch, and, if they want, take something away for tea and dinner."

"But why, ma'am?" Nina had whipped out her iPad and was already entering notes to herself even as she objected. "It is sad but it is nothing to do with us. Better we just help Aunty and Uncle Peters at their house. I can make for them one big pot of curry; anytime they are hungry, they can eat with rice or bread or naan."

Aunty Lee nodded at the food suggestion but said, "It is our business. Marianne and Laura had nothing to do with each other until the wine dining business. And that phone of Laura's was left outside my shop. Whether or not these people had something to do with what happened, they are part of this business now and they have to eat!"

The Peters family accepted Aunty Lee's offer and curry gratefully. Mycroft Peters brought over a note from his mother saying how touched she was.

"And she said we probably have enough plates and glasses and things. But if possible, you should bring your own helpers because the blasted maid has disappeared."

"Komal?" Aunty Lee remembered the small dark girl who had been with the Peters family for several years. "Did you make a report?"

"No. Not yet. The same day we got the news about my sister, she just took off. Father said she might have been scared by the police or superstitious about Marianne. Anyway, he said no point doing anything about it now, she may turn up in a couple of days. Until then we can manage on our own. Cherril is helping Mother take care of things."

"If we can be of any help . . . I could send Nina over. Here she has only got one old woman to look after."

"Thank you. I will let Mother know. Anyway, I should be getting back. The police are at our place looking through

Marianne's things. They seem to think she may have been seeing somebody without us knowing. We told them it was impossible, but I suppose they have to follow procedure. I think Mother asked me to bring her note over to get me out of the house in case I lost my temper with them and got arrested."

Aunty Lee looked thoughtful. "You used to have a temper. As a small boy."

"I suspect my mother thinks nothing has changed."

"And you?"

Mycroft paused. "I think Cherril has been good for me," he said, surprising Aunty Lee. "When I flare up about something and she doesn't understand why, she makes me explain it to her. In detail. Over and over until she understands why I'm angry. And by then I understand why I'm angry and somehow I'm not angry anymore."

Aunty Lee smiled to herself. Cherril Lim-Peters was smarter than she looked.

After Mycroft left, she told Nina, "I wish we could find that girl somehow."

"Do you think something happened to her too, ma'am?"

"I don't know. But I would like to make sure she is all right. Too many people are disappearing."

"Like her boss say maybe she is just scared by the police, so she run away? Where some people come from, the police are not like in Singapore."

Aunty Lee knew that was true. Sadly, she suspected Singapore police were not like their HD-TV American crime-solving colleagues. They were human beings without any supernatural or extrasensory abilities and they got tired and made mistakes. It was a good thing for all concerned, then, that Aunty Lee, whose investigative skills were ultra-developed from years of being *kaypoh* and who, being truly *kiasu*, never stopped just because she was tired, was coming into the game.

How Commissioner Raja had wished he was out of the game the day before. He and his wife had been friends with Professor Reginald and Mrs. Anne Peters for years. His children had been in school with theirs and he had known Marianne as a determined toddler, a Rollerblading tomboy, and the slightly chubby and sullen but still attractive young woman she had grown up into. Privately he had still thought her a child . . . and figured that once she found something or someone she was passionate about, she would surely shake off her malaise. But as it turned out, she had not lived long enough for that to happen.

Commissioner Raja knew there was nothing he could say to help her bereaved parents at this time. Even if they managed to find out who had brutally murdered their daughter, neither justice nor vengeance would bring Marianne back. But still, he had personally driven out to their house to deliver the news of her death. He felt it was the least he could do.

After the death of his wife, he and the Peters family had drifted apart somewhat, and seeing them again, he had been shocked by how much they had aged. When Professor Reginald Peters, chief and senior consultant of the department of cardiac, thoracic, and vascular surgery at the Yong Loo Lin School of Medicine, greeted him at the door, he looked at least twenty years older than when they last met two months back. He was gaunt, and tension from the self-control that kept him functioning had taken its toll. Suddenly he looked like an old man, slumped over and weak-looking, as though life had dealt him physical blows that left him barely able to stand. And his wife? Commissioner Raja had meant to build up to his news, but one look at his old friend told him he was wasting his time; the man already knew.

"No—" whispered Professor Peters.

"I'm sorry," said Commissioner Raja.

Professor Peters wept like a child, standing frozen and wailing, "No . . . no . . . no," out of a slack mouth without trying to wipe away his tears.

"Can you tell us anything more?" Anne Peters asked.

Commissioner Raja did not understand immediately what Mrs. Peters meant. Was she asking for an update on their investigation?

Anne Peters had been a beauty in her youth and had grown even more classically beautiful in her mature years. The shock and strain of Marianne's disappearance had left her looking brittle and frail, but she was still clearly in charge of herself and her home. Usually Commissioner Raja saw more beauty in large women. His late wife had been such a woman: large body, large heart, full lips, and generous with love and laughter. Even so many years after her death, Commissioner Raja compared all the women he met to her, and found each and every one of them lacking. But here, in Anne Peters, was pure Indian beauty of a different kind—high cheekbones, big sorrowful eyes, and slender, willowy strength. She smelled of fresh flowers he could not identify. Cologne? Soap? If she wore makeup, it was too discreetly applied to be noticed. She was the most beautiful woman he had ever seen. And at the moment she was watching Commissioner Raja as though his words were her only lifeline.

"Did my daughter suffer much?" she asked in a steady voice.

At this point in the investigation, Commissioner Raja had no idea. But he knew that however terrible Marianne Peters's earthly sufferings might have been, they were over now. Those of her family were only just beginning.

"No," he lied, trying to convince himself as much as her.

Anne Peters nodded. He saw she did not believe him. He also knew that he had given her the answer she wanted her husband to hear. It was for him that she had asked the question.

When Commissioner Raja phoned earlier to prepare them for his visit, his old friend had asked, "Is it Marianne?" Commissioner Raja said only that he would be there within half an hour. He was not trying to drag out the anguish, but in addition to the news of Marianne's death, he had questions he wanted to ask. Chief among them: Why hadn't they reported their daughter missing during the two weeks between her disappearance and the discovery of her body? Hadn't they suspected something was wrong when they hadn't heard from her for so long?

"Obviously somebody attacked her on the way to join her friends," Professor Peters said. "That's clearly what happened—she never managed to join them. I don't know why you are here asking us questions. You should go and question her friends, find out where they were supposed to meet up, why they never called when she didn't show up!"

"We had a bit of a disagreement just before Marianne left," Anne Peters interjected in a voice that sounded gentle and cultivated even in despair. "We thought she was punishing us by not getting in touch. We thought the best thing to do was leave her alone to get over the fight."

Commissioner Raja recognized Aunty Lee's maid when she came in wheeling a wire shopping cart packed full of supplies. Of course, even if he didn't recognize her, he might have identified her by the Aunty Lee's Delights T-shirt she was wearing. The bulging *tingkats* and plastic bags she was toting obviously contained enough to keep the Peters family going for some time. He had not thought he could be hungry at such a time, but the smell of hot oily cumin and chicken suddenly reminded him that he had missed lunch.

"You know Rosie?" Anne Peters asked. "M.L.'s wife. She lives just up the road. She's been such a great help to us."

"Of course I know Aunty Lee—" Referring to her as "Aunty" was to show that he was familiar with her business rather than out of respect for her age. He and Aunty Lee were actually contemporaries; Commissioner Raja's father had been a friend of the late M. L. Lee and had been one of those who'd initially been wary of him marrying this much younger woman. A fair man, he had later changed his mind. "She's helped me a couple of times too. I must tell my father she's still cooking."

Commissioner Raja recalled the case of the Nigerian gang that had tried to pull a scam using Mainland Chinese girls for cover in the early days of the Integrated Resorts Casino. Aunty Lee had picked them out as con artists immediately—she said it was because of their eating habits. Their greed at the buffet, taking far more than anyone could possibly eat just because they could, marked the women as unfamiliar with the lifestyle they were assuming. She had mentioned it to her husband, who had mentioned it to Raja, who had then been head of the Casino Regulatory Authority.

"She saved my image and saved the casino a lot of money once," he added.

Anne Peters smiled. "Funny, isn't it? You can be friends with people for years and not realize they know each other. Won't you join us for something to eat?" She lowered her voice. "Please do. Reginald hasn't eaten anything since last night. If you sit down with us, he may decide to sit down too, long enough to eat."

Commissioner Raja looked cautiously at his friend. He was well aware that in such circumstances the best-intentioned friends could be more a burden than a source of solace. But Anne Peters seemed serious and at the moment her husband did not look as though he were aware of much of anything going on around him at all.

"Nina says Rosie told her to stay as long as we need her," Anne Peters continued. "I told her we will be fine since they'll be here to help with things when . . . well, you haven't been able to tell us when we can make arrangements for Marianne."

"Well, we had a bit of maid trouble," Professor Peters cut in as though in response to a question. As long as his daughter's body was not in the house, he did not have to face what had happened. "The girl just disappeared. Right after news about . . . Marianne . . . came out. Didn't give any reason. We had no reason to think she was unhappy, she just upped and left."

Commissioner Raja frowned. "You mean she's also missing?"

"She ran off," Anne Peters said dully. "She's not missing."

"So you do know where she is?"

Commissioner Raja looked at their blank faces. He did not mean to hound them. He had just told his good friends that their beloved daughter was dead. But he was also a policeman. He looked to Aunty Lee's maid, who had finished setting up a buffet-style arrangement on the counter: chicken and potato curry, braised vegetables and steamed rice, with bottles of *achar*, *ikan bilis* with peanuts, and sambal. Nina had placed serving spoons and a stack of clean plates and cutlery at the end of the row.

"Do you know where their servant could have gone?" Commissioner Raja asked Nina. He was not sure why he asked. But she worked for a friend in the same estate and was clearly familiar with the Peterses' household.

"No, sir. My boss ask me already. She also want to know."

"I see." Cowardly or tactfully, Raja decided to leave the question to her. "Tell your boss if she finds out anything, come and tell me. Tell her don't go and do her crazy things, okay? This is serious, not play play."

"Yes, sir."

"Could Komal have seen who took Marianne?" Anne Peters asked. "She did disappear almost immediately after Marianne—"

"Komal wouldn't have seen anything," Professor Peters said. "Even if she saw something, she wouldn't have known it. Anyway she didn't disappear immediately after Marianne. If this crazy story is true, Marianne disappeared over two weeks ago. Those girls she was supposed to be traveling with say they never saw her!" Almost casually he picked up a small crystal vase and smashed it against the wall. His wife did not flinch. She looked as though she was beyond flinching. Discreetly, Nina got a pan and brush and started clearing up the shards.

"She was a good girl," Anne Peters said. There was a

quiver in her voice, but she spoke with quiet determination. "Komal spoke Hindi and Sindhi but not much English. She and Marianne hardly had anything to do with
each other. She didn't have anything to do with this." She
set her lips grimly. "Komal must have been seeing somebody. I didn't want to believe it of her. I ignored all the
people who warned me to keep strict controls. I wanted
to respect her, but look at what she did, right when we
needed her most." There was a hurt betrayal in her voice
that came from more than her feelings about their maid's
abandonment of them.

Nina, who had returned to the room after emptying
the dustpan, had remained by the kitchen door while
Anne Peters was speaking. Now she went over to where
Mrs. Peters was sitting with Commissioner Raja. Professor
Peters was still pacing around the room.

"I have cleaned up the kitchen. If it is all right, I will go
and clean upstairs and do the laundry, then tomorrow I
will cook things and bring over."

Anne Peters glanced at her husband, but he was beyond
caring about household arrangements. "Thank you," she
said. "Thank you very much. That would help us very
much. But don't worry about cooking. We can phone for
something. And Mycroft and Cherril will be back soon."

"Let her prepare something simple for you," Commissioner Raja advised. "At a time like this, you don't want to
be eating pizza and fried chicken." And from experience

he knew that at a time of bereavement, clean bedsheets and clear soups did more good than condolence notices and floral wreaths.

Finally leaving the Peterses', Commissioner Raja told his driver to pull up alongside a property fronted by a long, low white picket fence before they reached the main road.

Aunty Lee was out her front door and coming down the drive before Commissioner Raja's driver turned off the engine.

"Then why did Komal run away?" Aunty Lee demanded of Commissioner Raja before the commissioner had fully gotten himself out of the car. "She must have had something to do with it even if they didn't leave together. The girl didn't know anybody in Singapore. When they tried to give her Sundays off, she didn't want them because she had nowhere to go. Don't worry, they were not taking advantage of her. They were giving her thirty dollars for every Sunday she stayed in the house, even when there was no work for her to do. But if she didn't know anybody here and didn't want to go out on Sundays, why did she suddenly pack up and run away? How could she pack up and run away without a trace?"

"They knew her better than anyone else. If they say she ran away . . ." Commissioner Raja shrugged. He knew some maids had very good reasons for running away from their employers. Right now he didn't want to go into why the Peterses were so certain Komal had run away from them.

They were friends and they were good people, but they were also under extreme stress. Without admitting what he thought, even to himself, he hoped they would make it up to the girl when she came back safely.

"How are they taking it up there? What do they think happened?"

"They think someone attacked Marianne en route to join her friends. They blame her friends for not raising the alarm sooner."

"Is that the official view?"

Commissioner Raja shrugged again. It was not that he did not trust Aunty Lee, just that there was no such thing as an official view, only the official report. And the official report had not been issued yet.

"If that was the case, why did Komal disappear? And did she take her things? Did she take any other things with her?"

"I don't think the Peterses are in any state to notice what the girl took. They didn't mention anything missing."

"Sometimes these little girls are afraid of talking to the police," Aunty Lee said absentmindedly. "Nothing at all to do with your people here, of course, but you don't know what it might be like where they come from. I've asked Nina to see what she can find out for me."

"I thought you might," Commissioner Raja said. "But you realize, of course, that anything she says . . ."

Aunty Lee managed to smile and look grim at the same time. "She is also a poor young girl. I just want to make sure she is not also dead somewhere in the sea because that is where girls seem to be showing up these days. Anyway, I have to get to my shop. You can give me a lift out. Your suspects are all coming to eat at my place. Do you want to come in for a drink?"

"Be careful," Commissioner Raja said. "Something funny is going on."

"Exactly," Aunty Lee said. "That's why I need help from you and that nice man Salim."

"You need our help?"

"Sometimes a bit of uniform and authority is enough to make people behave. If not, it is always good to have a strong man around."

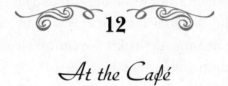

12

At the Café

Aunty Lee was not just *kaypoh*. She was driven by a compulsion to know that was as strong or stronger than hunger.

"So I thought, since you have to stay in Singapore longer than you expected, why not come and eat at my place?" Aunty Lee had suggested as though it had just occurred to her, and she had picked up the phone to call her prospective guests immediately. "At my café, I mean. I'm closing it to customers temporarily, so it will be my treat, of course. If you miss your food from back home, I am sure I can come up with something."

Frank Cunningham, who had taken the call, relayed Aunty Lee's invitation to his wife. The Cunninghams looked at each other. Though they were not hard up by any stretch of the imagination, this extended stay in the island city had thrown their travel budget off balance. New travel and hotel arrangements could be made, of course, but though the Raffles was a most understanding and accommodating hotel, it was not cheap. And their current frame of mind was far from adventurous. When Aunty Lee's invitation came, they had been living almost completely on familiar and easily available fast foods.

Lucy gestured to her husband to cover the mouthpiece of the phone before saying, "Why not?"

"What does she want from us? There's no such thing as a free lunch."

"What does it matter? We have nothing to hide. Besides, it's like the birds of the field, neither sowing nor reaping, but the Lord provides."

"Nothing like free food, eh?" Harry Sullivan said to no one in particular as he watched the Cunninghams come into Aunty Lee's Delights. The couple did not laugh.

"We'll pay you what it's worth," Frank said to Aunty Lee. "Though seeing you've closed your shop, you wouldn't be wanting to charge us your regular rates."

"The police got you to close down, did they?" Harry asked. "We can't leave the country and you can't run your business." He seemed genuinely concerned. "That's not very fair to you, is it? It's not just a matter of what you would be taking in today, this week, and so on. It's what your customers are going to think. And the chaps who turn up and think you're closed for good."

"We just don't really know where else to go. There are stalls, of course, but we don't know how clean everything is—it's Asia after all. And we were supposed to get our yellow fever vaccinations before coming out, but we never did," Lucy worried. "Of course, we would like to pay you—please let us."

They were looking less and less like a well-traveled tourist couple out to see the world.

"Don't be silly," Aunty Lee said in the manner of a motherly old lady. "I like having you people around. No, the police didn't tell us to shut down. With everything that's been going on, I didn't want people coming in here out of curiosity, if you know what I mean—"

It was clear that the others—Lucy Cunningham at least—knew what she meant. "It's so dreadful, isn't it? We've never been mixed up in anything like this before. Now every time I leave our room, I can feel people looking at us, wondering whether we had anything to do with the murders."

"I told you that's ridiculous," Frank said with a trace of impatience. "You're imagining things. Nobody even knows who we are."

"Our names were in the papers—they'll recognize them from the register. And even if the hotel people don't, he will . . . We should have left as soon as we found out that Laura Kwee wasn't here!"

Genteelly helping the distraught Lucy to some slices of fried cold cuts (luncheon meat barely qualified as food in Aunty Lee's book, but she had guessed correctly that cold cuts and bottled ketchup represented comfort food to her guests), Aunty Lee pounced. She had been waiting for this.

"Poor Laura Kwee. So sad. Did you know her well?"

"Oh, we never met her. She sent us an e-mail, didn't she, Frank? That's how we got to know her. We were going to meet her for the first time that night, that terrible night, but of course she never showed up—"

"Lucy!" Frank's voice was low but absolute in its command to silence.

His wife, startled, stared at him. Then, with the advantage a long marriage brings to the least discerning, she saw what he was thinking. "No. You can't think so. He wouldn't have—you can't say that. You can't even think that!"

"He's not the only one mixed up in the business now."

Though this exchange told Aunty Lee nothing, apparently it was enough for Lucy Cunningham. All Aunty Lee could gather was that the Cunninghams had indeed been invited by Laura Kwee for more reasons than to sample Aunty Lee's good food, but she was not offended. She was determined to find out what those reasons were.

"And you, Mr. Sullivan. You also had an appointment to meet with Laura Kwee here in my shop?"

This made both Cunninghams turn to study Harry Sullivan with great interest. Though perhaps they were still trying to figure out why he looked familiar.

"Hey, no fair. You're supposed to call me Harry, re- member? This 'Mr. Sullivan' business makes me feel like I should be in a suit and tie! And no. It was her friend Selina I ran into first. We had a common interest in wine and she told me about this project of her husband's. And I thought, why not? I could do with a couple of good meals in good company. Pity about those poor girls. Wish I'd had a chance to get to know them better."

"I thought you were getting along rather well." Aunty Lee smiled. "Laura was helping you write your articles for that magazine, right?"

"I have no idea what you're talking about," Harry said. Then, because it was clear that Aunty Lee did know what she was talking about, "It was just a joke. She got a kick out of being a secret reviewer, you know, getting inside informa- tion and so on." Aunty Lee nodded without commenting.

"Have you been in touch with your relatives back home? When will they start getting worried that you haven't shown up? Do you have any children?"

"No," said Frank Cunningham at the same time his wife said, "He's back in Sydney." The reproachful looks they directed at each other were almost identical.

"That's the kind of thing Laura Kwee would know," Aunty Lee said. "She liked knowing everything about ev- erybody. And she was very systematic. Almost paranoid, and she kept track of everything. It's all probably on the computer."

The Cunninghams seemed very interested in this.

"Maybe it's just as well," Lucy Cunningham said. "The Good Lord has His way of arranging things. Where is her computer? She was looking up some information for us. Maybe it's on her computer. We already paid her, so it should be all right for us to look at what she found out, right?" Her husband didn't look as though he agreed, but he said nothing.

"She had it with her the last time she was here," Aunty Lee remembered aloud. "She had to leave it behind because she couldn't manage to carry all her things home with her. Unless she came back to pick it up later. I must ask Nina."

In the pause that followed this, Frank told Harry that the Cunninghams definitely remembered meeting a Harry Sullivan on their travels. They could not remember where, but that's where they knew the name from.

"Nothing to be ashamed of," Frank went on, "not seeing eye to eye with all your family, boy. The thing is don't let that keep you away from them. Family is family. Lucy and me, we know that only too well right now, don't we, Mums?"

Harry Sullivan shook his head, not even bothering to answer. "I know that white men are supposed to think all Asians look the same," he said to Aunty Lee. "Now in this case, you've got a white man that thinks all white men look the same!"

"You're right, you know," Lucy said. "There's something at the back of my mind too, only I can't pinpoint it . . ."

"Hello." Carla Saito appeared. She was wearing a black shirt and black jeans—probably the same ones she had been wearing when she was first at the café. But without makeup or jewelry other than a large man's watch, she could have been a different person. She paused just inside the doorway and looked at the others. No one moved. Aunty Lee looked around the table. It was almost as though the people seated there were afraid of Carla. The two Cunninghams leaned into each other as though shrinking away from a threat.

"Please join us," Aunty Lee invited. "We'll be eating soon."

"I'm not hungry," Carla announced. "So what have we found out? The sooner this is over, the sooner we can all get out of Singapore, right?"

"You've all just been through a traumatic experience," Aunty Lee prompted. "You take it easy, maybe what you are trying to remember will come back to you."

"Don't you want children?" Lucy Cunningham suddenly asked Carla Saito. The expression on her face was like the one Aunty Lee had seen on Nina's when Nina was expressing her disapproval of lesbians.

"Do you have children?" Carla asked her in turn.

Aunty Lee was struck by a sudden insight—two in fact. The first: Carla Saito did want children. The second: Lucy Cunningham had recently lost a son or daughter and was grieving. This was confirmed when Frank Cunningham cut in with, "Hey, you're getting a little too personal here!"

When Carla gave his wife a long look and fell silent, Aunty Lee knew the younger woman had picked up on it too.

"Maybe you'll just give me a hand in the kitchen?" Aunty Lee had read her visitors well. Lucy Cunningham rose to join her immediately.

Carla said, "I wouldn't be any use to you," and the two men assumed her words were not meant for them.

"But there are certain standards, certain rules of behavior, that everyone accepts," Lucy said once they were in the kitchen. As Aunty Lee had guessed, Mrs. Cunningham was much more at ease once she had something to busy her hands with. Now she was peeling shallots (with a swift, practiced skill that made Aunty Lee look on her with more respect) and away from her husband. "People know what's right. And what's wrong. Everybody agrees on that."

"But how do you know everybody agrees?" Aunty Lee asked, seemingly intent on washing mustard greens in one of the sinks. She squinted and picked out what might have been a bug or dirt or a specimen of plant life not developed along consumer-advocate guidelines.

"It's obvious, isn't it? The people you talk to, it's in the papers. It's just normal, good, human values."

There had been a slight waver before she said "human," as though Lucy had had to make a quick substitution for another, less neutral word.

"God made us all individuals," Aunty Lee observed.

"God gave us rules to live by," Lucy Cunningham said quietly. Again she was on guard, focused on her shallots.

Aunty Lee did not learn anything throughout the rest of the meal. She fed her visitors well, with a huge platter of vegetarian fried rice, sambal long beans, and, of course, *achar* and *kropok*. It was a simple meal and easily put together, but it was good.

Harry Sullivan left first. It was getting on to the rush hour by the time the Cunninghams were ready to leave Aunty Lee's Delights. Sometime around 5 p.m., Aunty Lee told the police later. She saw their taxi arrive through the front window and stopped only to switch off the burner beneath the teapot before going out to see them off. The evening dusk was settling, but the night-lights had not yet come on. Frank Cunningham paused, half into the taxi, already telling the taxi driver some story about his and his wife's travels. Lucy, still on the sidewalk, lit up at the sight of Aunty Lee.

"Please remember," she said. "When you find Laura Kwee's computer, we would like to see it. I remember the last thing she said was that she had news for us. She definitely found out something and it had to do with someone who would be here at your shop for dinner that night—"

It was at that moment when something seemed to crash and explode right beside her. Lucy screamed, burning. There was a second explosion and flames leaped up around Frank in the taxi. Aunty Lee stumbled, thrown aside as someone pushed roughly past her.

"It's the damned perverts!" Frank Cunningham shouted. "They know we're on their tail! Damn them!"

"Call the nine-nine-nine!" Aunty Lee shouted. She threw a thick sofa quilt over Lucy and was trying to find something to cover Frank with, and then suddenly Salim was there, spraying water everywhere, yanking the hose, already switched on full blast. "Get ambulance and police here!"

"Already called," Salim shouted back.

"What are you doing here?"

"Keeping an eye on things. Don't want another body showing up." He was looking around at the chaotic scene; people running around, people standing and staring, Lucy Cunningham wailing, and Frank Cunningham calling everyone who tried to help him a pervert. "Where's Nina?"

Then suddenly Harry Sullivan appeared, waving some kind of rod, and attacked Salim. "You're a terrorist! You're one of those fundies that goes around bombing people like us!"

Salim simply—almost gracefully—avoided the tire iron Harry Sullivan was whacking in his direction. He removed the metal tool and gently pinned the large man, still shouting, onto the ground.

Aunty Lee went to stand beside Salim. "If you stop struggling, I'm sure he will let you go. Won't you, Senior Staff Sergeant?" Then, as the policeman relaxed his grip, "Are you all right? I thought you already left, Mr. Sullivan."

"Traffic was slow. I saw the explosion, the fire, and I saw him—" Harry pointed at Salim. "He was standing there watching. You can't trust him just because he's a policeman. Police can be the worst of all. They think they're gods and can get away with anything! He could have tricked Marianne into going off with him. Who better to trust than a uniform?"

That was true, Aunty Lee reflected. She didn't know. But she was impressed by how swiftly Salim had disarmed Harry Sullivan without hurting him. "Why are you here?" she asked SSS Salim. "Alone in the dark? Were you watching the shop?"

"Just looking around," SSS Salim said. "I was on my way home. I'm off duty."

Harry Sullivan snorted. Aunty Lee looked thoughtful.

The fire was put out and the Cunninghams declared safe and sound though traumatized and sent to a hospital for examination. Aunty Lee's questions would have to wait.

"Will you see me safely back to my house, young man? Nina's there, so once I'm there, I will be all right."

"Of course," said SSS Salim.

Harry Sullivan was obviously displeased, though Aunty Lee could not tell whether this was because he was worried for her safety.

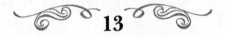

13

Waiting Room

The Cunninghams were kept overnight in the hospital and treated for shock and minor burns. Frank had a broken arm, and Aunty Lee went to see him first so that she could tell Lucy how he was. And also so she could spend more time with Lucy.

"Tell me why you and Frank are in Singapore, dear," Aunty Lee began. "Do you remember what you said just before the explosion?" she asked. Lucy shook her head. She looked exhausted and resigned.

"I don't know. I don't care. I'm just so tired."

"Do you need anything?"

"Oh no. We're very well looked after here."

"Is there anyone I can call for you? Who should know you are here?"

Lucy shook her head. "We're both going to be all right, they said . . . ?"

"Oh yes. It's just that if anybody tries to reach you and gets worried . . ."

Lucy Cunningham motioned for her purse and wrote something in her notebook before tearing out the page to pass to Aunty Lee.

"It's not really a secret, but please don't mention it to my husband yet. Just call this number and tell him that Frank and Lucy Cunningham are in hospital here. And please tell him we're all right. Don't tell him to come to see us or anything, just let him know where we are. I think he should know."

"Who is the message for?"

"Joe, of course. Joseph Cunningham."

It was a local number, Aunty Lee saw. "Of course I will."

"But don't tell Frank. I'm not asking you to do anything wrong, but please . . . don't tell Frank."

"It was a turpentine bomb," SSS Salim said to Commissioner Raja. "Two of them. I would say an amateur job. Luckily not that much damage was done. We are trying to track down the source of the materials, but . . ." It was not necessary to point out how common the solvent was in a city that was constantly painting and varnishing cars and buildings.

Returning to the station after seeing Aunty Lee safely back home, Salim had gotten caught up in writing up the events of the night and reading through his case notes. He was still at his desk when the morning shift came on duty and he received the call summoning him to the commissioner's office at the district HQ as soon as possible. In Singapore, no place was more than half an hour away in light traffic, but he decided not to risk going home to change, just in case.

When he put his report on the commissioner's desk, he was certain that he had managed to include all the vital details. He had already talked to everyone present at the scene, except the Cunninghams, who had been taken to the hospital. Salim had been off duty when the incident occurred and wondered if he was going to get into trouble for hanging around the café on his own. Of course, there was no reason why he could not go anywhere he wanted during his off time, and his hunch that something was going to happen in the vicinity of the café had paid off . . . but going into headquarters unshaven and wearing a grimy green polo shirt and jeans made him feel unprepared and somehow guilty. He wondered whether he would be reprimanded, perhaps even suspended and demoted.

Why hadn't he dashed home to shower and change? Now that the incident was over, what could be so urgent about getting his report together before going to see the commissioner? People in authority always asked for things to be done immediately, but they did not expect you to take them seriously. Or had the Caucasian man who attacked him made a complaint? Foreigners were always quick to shout "police brutality" even when the aggression and brutality had come from them.

According to the report from the hospital, the Cunninghams had both suffered second-degree burns, which they would probably have considered terrible enough . . . unless you considered how much worse it might have been if not for SSS Salim's quick actions. Commissioner Raja was of the opinion that the Cunninghams had been very lucky.

"Homemade bombs?"

"Yes, sir. There was a space of time between the first and second explosion, so I would say there was only one guy responsible. Otherwise they could have attacked at the same time."

The bombs had been basic Molotov cocktails: glass bottles filled with turpentine and plugged with cloth wicks that had been lit. Despite Aunty Lee's faith in criminal forensics, the police had not been able to recover any fingerprints from what was left of the bombs.

"And I hear you were accused of being a terrorist?"

"What? Oh. No, sir. The gentleman was in shock. He apologized later. He said he just saw me and panicked."

Commissioner Raja nodded. Neither he nor Salim mentioned that racial stereotyping had probably contributed to Harry Sullivan's mistake. There was more than enough of that being done maliciously.

"And you disarmed him with magic . . ."

"Sir?"

"That is what the Australian lady claims in her statement. She said he rushed toward you with a stick, but you just held out your hand and Mr. Sullivan fell down."

"*Silat*, sir. Energy that emits outward from the center line is defensive. I blocked him and his own offensive energy moved backward into his body."

Commissioner Raja nodded again. Salim did not think this was a good time to ask if he believed him. He also didn't know Commissioner Raja was thinking it was a pity this was not the best time to discuss incorporating *silat* into basic combat training.

"You are currently the officer in charge of the Bukit Tinggi Neighbourhood Police Post, right?"

Salim nodded. He was suddenly very tired. He also felt thirsty and hungry and wondered fleetingly when Aunty Lee would be opening her café for customers again. He would probably have all the time in the world to eat there once the commissioner had finished firing him. If only he didn't also end up with a disciplinary hearing. But then once he was fired, he could hardly spend his money on eating out at expensive cafés. He had no idea how much Aunty Lee's Delights charged for their meals since Aunty Lee had refused to let him pay up till now, but after he lost his job he knew that would not continue.

"Do you have someone you can appoint to take charge temporarily at Bukit Tinggi?"

"Yes, sir. Officer Pang," Salim said. So, he was being

suspended, then. "I mean in the normal course of things, Officer Pang would handle things, but right now, with everything going on . . ." Suddenly he forgot how tired he was. "Right now it's complicated. I would need more time to brief him." There were so many things going on in the peaceful little neighborhood that he wanted to get to the bottom of it all himself.

"Good. I am appointing you temporarily to the CID. You will be serving under your old jurisdiction, but I want you to report directly to me."

SSS Salim nodded again. The main thing was that he still seemed to have a job. "Why?" he asked, without meaning to. He was not questioning the commissioner's decision, just trying to understand it.

Commissioner Raja managed to keep his face impassive. "Mrs. M. L. Lee phoned. I believe you two have met before. She seems to have formed a good opinion of you, said you saved the lives of those people and without you there her shop would have burned down."

"Actually there was no real danger of that happening, sir." SSS Salim felt he had to point this out.

The commissioner nodded his approval of the comment but continued as though Salim had not spoken. "Nonetheless she is nervous after all the things that have happened. She seems to have confidence in you, and she asked that we appoint you to keep an eye on things. Also she is the wife of an old friend and alone in the world now. We don't want anything to happen to her."

SSS Salim could understand the commissioner's concern . . . although it seemed to him that there were few people less alone in the world than Aunty Lee, and he could not imagine her feeling nervous about anything. But he knew that the commissioner had just given him the opportunity that could make or break his career, so he kept his thoughts to himself.

"Go and get the statements of those people in hospital and make sure that Mrs. Lee is all right. Understood?"

"One more thing, sir."

"Yes, Salim?"

"I don't know if it is relevant to the case. But I heard that Mrs. Cunningham was calling to someone to call Joe for her. Perhaps you better find out who this Joe is."

When he left the commissioner's office, Salim felt much less tired than he'd felt when he went in. His career was not dead and life was full of possibilities again, but he had no idea where to go from here. His phone buzzed—he had put it on silent mode before going into Commissioner Raja's office—and when he saw the call was from Aunty Lee, he answered it right there in the corridor. He was not sure whether to thank her for saving his job, but before he could say more than "Hello, Mrs. Lee—"

"We've found Komal," Aunty Lee said. "The Peters family's missing helper, remember? She wouldn't have run away for nothing!

"And I think I know what the Cunninghams' secret is," Aunty Lee announced proudly. "Or rather we will all see soon—you too if you go round to the hospital. And you should know about the e-mails that Laura Kwee had been sending Marianne and the Cunninghams too. Carla Saito should have told you about them earlier . . . Because you see, the key to all this is Laura Kwee. The sort of person Laura Kwee was. How soon can you get to my shop? I want to show you everything before you drive me to the hospital!"

SSS Salim was a bit overwhelmed. When he arrived, Aunty Lee insisted on ushering him into her café, though it was still closed. Aunty Lee said it was officially because of the damage caused by the fire. Unofficially because too many people were coming out of curiosity to see the damage, and serving them took up too much time. "After all, for now this is our headquarters," she said. "We can't have people walking in and out nonstop."

Salim wondered about customer loyalty. But after all, that was Aunty Lee's business (in every sense). Either she knew her customers well enough to know they would return or this was an issue she simply didn't have to worry about. It must be nice to be rich enough not to worry about such things.

"Everybody has secrets," Aunty Lee said. "That poor girl Komal, for instance. She is so scared of her employers, she is scared of the police. Even if she has done nothing worse than eating leftovers, she is scared. But I can talk to her. Everybody hides something, so they seem suspicious. But some of these things are going to be innocent stupid things like women trying to lose weight but eating peach cake secretly. So we have to rule out the innocent secrets, and when we have done that, we will know who is responsible for these terrible crimes!"

It sounded very simple. Salim felt he ought to warn her that this was not how things were done in Singapore, but when he tried—

"Nonsense," she exclaimed. "This is how problems are solved all over the world! Now the secrets. Nina, can you write them on the board for Salim, please?"

The board was the one on which the daily specials were written.

> **The Cunninghams:** *Not wanting to say why they are in Singapore. Lucy Cunningham seems to be hiding something.*
> **Mycroft Peters:** *Not reporting his sister missing. Seems more eager to move on from her murder than solve it.*
> **Cherril Lim-Peters:** *Is she interested in starting a business with Mark or simply interested in Mark?*
> **Carla Saito:** *What really happened between her and Marianne Peters that she doesn't want to tell us about?*
> **Mark Lee:** *What is the secret he and Laura Kwee shared, that she threatened him with revealing?*

"Is that all?" SSS Salim asked. He was joking, but Aunty Lee took him seriously.

"Well, we should include Harry Sullivan because he was

here on all the wine dining nights. But though the man has his own issues, I'm not sure he keeps them secret . . ."

From what SSS Salim had seen of the man, he had to agree. Mr. Sullivan had made clear what he thought of nonwhite people as well as what he thought of other white people who didn't hold themselves up to his standards—the Cunninghams, for example. What had he said? That they were living off the fat of the land with no thought for their children, which was not surprising because—

"Harry Sullivan seems to think the Cunninghams have something to hide."

"For example, I'm sure you have secrets," Aunty Lee said confidently. She was not just teasing the young man. She had sensed how he and Nina looked at each other—probably before they were aware of it themselves.

"No," SSS Salim said.

The plan Aunty Lee drew up:

Find out who the damned pervert is that Frank Cunningham thought was after them.

Find out about Laura's relationships and mysterious phone calls.

Obtain copies of Marianne's e-mails from Carla Saito.

Get the Peterses to talk about Marianne.

"Is all this enough to start with?"

"Plenty."

"Of course, if you are too busy with your own leads, I can follow up on these myself."

"Not at all."

"Now you better get home and have a shower and a rest. I want to go to the hospital and then talk to Komal."

When Salim left for home, he again had that feeling of being looked after. He had lived alone since his return to Singapore. The grandmother who had brought him up had died right after he graduated, almost as though she had been waiting for her long lifetime of responsibility to be over. There were times when he stayed on longer at work than he need have, just as he had once stayed late in school, simply to avoid going back to the empty rooms.

As he was leaving the café, Nina came in from the back and passed him a flimsy red plastic bag, the sort people used to carry fresh fruit bought off market stalls.

"Money plant," she said. "It's very tough. If you don't have a flowerpot, put it in water and it will grow. Better still, put it in a bowl near the window."

"Mosquitoes . . ." SSS Salim said automatically. But he took the bag.

"Then get fish," Nina said firmly. "Those small fish, fifty cents each. Then, when you go home, you won't be alone."

It touched him that she had not forgotten what he barely remembered saying.

Aunty Lee was still staring at the chart when Nina returned from seeing Salim off.

"All the ingredients here. We just have to put them together the right way," Aunty Lee said. "But first I need to do a bit of research. You said you found Laura Kwee's laptop, right?"

"I already looked at it," Nina said, unabashed. "I was looking for the guest and payment list for the wine dining, but there's nothing."

"Then do me a favor. Laura was helping me by writing about my café and products. I just want to make sure nobody tries to reach her through her sites and links. Can you get me in to look at her connections on her computer?"

"You can do that from your own computer, ma'am."

"But it would be so much easier from Laura's, right? Because she would have set up all the name lists and who has paid and who has not? If you like, I will get in touch with her family and ask them—plus Laura was so lazy and secretive she is sure to have some complicated passwords and then have lists of her passwords. If we can get hold of that, it will be so much easier."

"Now I'm going to take a look around the employment agencies. Don't look so worried, Nina. After sharing all my secrets with you, I'm not going to let you go so easily."

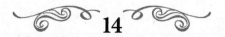

14

Collecting Ingredients

Aunty Lee had a knack for preparing foods people swore tasted exactly as they remembered them from their distant childhoods. She was frequently asked for recipes and accused of withholding vital ingredients when these did not produce the desired result. In truth, she withheld nothing, but she could not give instructions for instinct. That had to be developed over years of experience. Ingredients today were either far purer or diluted with very different kinds of impurities than they had been when Aunty Lee was learning to cook. And the taste buds of those she cooked for were less sensitive as the people grew older.

When cooking, you had to make allowances and adjustments to compensate for all these changes.

Moreover, Aunty Lee knew how important it was not only to know your ingredients but also to know the people you were dealing with. She kept that in mind when trying to figure out "human recipes."

While the Cunninghams were recuperating in hospital, the Peterses' runaway maid had been found. Aunty Lee could not claim credit for this.

Nina had finally managed to track down Komal Chandani. She could not have done it without her vast network of friends, their relatives, friends of their relatives, and so on. Aunty Lee was very impressed. She had lived in Singapore all her life, while Nina had been there all of seven years, but when it came to having contacts in helpful places, nobody was better than Nina. Until this talent of Nina's surfaced, Aunty Lee had been limited to counting on taxi-driver and Tai-Tai networks for information. This had always involved taking more taxi rides and attending more charity dinners than Aunty Lee was happy with.

When she got home from the café, she found Nina and SSS Salim in her living room along with a small, dark, frightened-looking girl.

"Should we get an interpreter?" SSS Salim asked.

"Afterward, if you want to take a proper statement. For now, just listen. She can understand us. Right, Komal? You can understand?"

Komal looked scared, but she nodded.

"Do you know what happened to Miss Marianne?" Aunty Lee asked gently.

Komal shook her head. Then she nodded—and shook her head again. "Don't know," she said.

"You know she's dead?"

A nod.

"But you don't know what happened?"

Another nod, with relief this time. "I try to help Miss Mari."

"How did you try to help her?"

"I pack her things in her bag for her."

"What things?"

"Things to wear. Passport."

"Why didn't Miss Mari pack them herself?"

"She go already. She go first. Then her man, he says she needs her things. She don't want to come back because if she comes back, then her father don't let her go. So she ask her man to come and get her bag for her."

"Then?"

"Then, when I bring for him the bag, he give me fifty dollars. He say it is from Miss Mari and I must not tell anybody or her family will be very angry with her and with me."

"Did you believe that?"

Komal nodded earnestly. "Then, when Miss Mari is dead, I am scared. That is why I run away. I never take anything, I swear, madam!"

"I also made phone call to Carla Saito, ma'am," Nina put in. "I said if she wants to talk to Miss Marianne's maid, she should come here. I hope that is all right."

Aunty Lee was surprised. "It's all right. But I thought you didn't like Carla Saito."

Nina looked uncomfortable. "Ma'am, it is not for me to like or not like. But Komal said that Miss Marianne talked about Carla Saito. And she wish for Carla Saito to meet her family. Ma'am, I thought since you know Mr. and Mrs. Peters . . ."

Komal looked hopeful, as Nina left her words open to interpretation. Aunty Lee did not think it a good idea to introduce her old friends to someone whom the Peterses would probably see as the cause of their present tragedy. But it was clearly something that little Komal had set her heart on. Aunty Lee looked at Nina's mutely pleading expression and guessed the leverage she had used to get Komal to come back to Binjai Park.

"You think it would make Miss Marianne happy?"

"Yes, please, madam! It is the last thing I can do for Miss Marianne."

"Remember what Marianne told Carla Saito about the guy planning a romantic getaway for two weeks? And then the young couple that found Laura Kwee's body? They just got married and had their wedding dinner at the hotel the night before. Suppose it's the same place. They were staying in a chalet, right? Find out more about that resort where they were staying, Nina. And I should be getting over to the hospital soon. Where is Carla Saito?"

Sometimes pieces just fell into place, Aunty Lee thought, as the phone and doorbell rang simultaneously. Aunty Lee answered the phone and Nina let Carla in.

"Yes. Shall we come over now?"

"I'm glad you came," Aunty Lee said to Carla Saito. "Because there is someone else who wants to meet you."

Carla knew where the Peters house was. She had been on the street outside it before, and had spent quite some time staring at it from across the road without attempting to go inside.

"I thought they were keeping Marianne prisoner in there," she admitted. "I know it sounds stupid now. But at the time I remember Marianne saying how traditional and protective her parents were and I thought there was a good chance—or rather I hoped that's where she was."

An old black dog who had flopped down in the drive lifted his head hopefully as the gate opened.

"Hey, Chewy," Carla said, and the dog thumped its tail politely but unenthusiastically. Clearly they were not who he was hoping to see.

"You know Chewy?"

"Marianne told me about Chewbacca. He was her dog for sixteen years; when they got him he was so small and scared she used to smuggle him in to sleep in her bed even though he wasn't supposed to be inside the house. I think one of the reasons she wanted to come back here was to see Chewy."

Aunty Lee had explained simply that she and a friend of Marianne's had located Komal and were bringing her back. Komal had been frightened and still was; and "the friend" of Marianne's wanted to talk to both Komal and her mistress.

Anne Peters looked at Carla Saito for so long without speaking that Aunty Lee wondered whether she had made a mistake in bringing her here.

Then Anne Peters said to Carla, "I think I always knew at some level. But you know what it is like being a minority. Even after we have been here for so many years. It would just have been one more thing to make her life more difficult. If she were here right now, we would be fighting about it. I would not approve because I am her mother and it is my job not to approve."

"She kept saying it would have broken your heart, that you would never have approved," Carla Saito said. She was daring Mrs. Peters to contradict her. She could not feel sorry for this woman who had been the cause of so much of Marianne's unhappiness.

"It is my job to protect her from other people. But what can I do now?"

Carla said, "You can change other people."

"I would not have approved. But it is wrong of you to say I would never have approved. Did Marianne tell you I was against my son marrying Cherril?"

Carla was confused by the change of subject. "She never mentioned that. But I remember her saying she was glad Cherril was around because you had someone to do stuff like shopping and manicures with. She hated stuff like that."

"I always thought Marianne was a bit jealous. Cherril was Chinese and from a broken home. She was a flight attendant without a university degree. Please listen and let me finish—" She held up a hand as Carla started to interrupt. "I didn't approve because making a marriage work between two different personalities is difficult enough without adding two different backgrounds. And it was my duty as a mother to make potential difficulties clear to them. But once they were married, it was my duty as a mother to stand by them."

"Marianne didn't like Cherril. She said she didn't know what Mycroft saw in her. She said you didn't like her either, but you were pretending to because you wanted to have grandchildren."

"It's true. I didn't like Cherril before she married my son. Now they are married it's irrelevant whether I like her or not because she is family."

Carla Saito waited.

Anne Peters went on: "You would have become family

too, given time. I want you to know that." That was why she had shared her initial reaction to Cherril Lim with Carla. It was something Marianne would have appreciated, Carla thought.

"The shock is still too strong. I know she is dead and I should feel worse. But she's been away so much I still keep expecting to get another text message from her saying where she is now."

"When did she send that last message?" Aunty Lee asked sharply. "And where is her phone? And her computer?"

She had been silent for so long that they had almost forgotten she was there.

"Marianne's laptop is missing. Komal said she asked for it, which is strange because Marianne usually used the computer at work or her iPhone. The laptop was several years old and she hardly used it. And though she asked for her laptop, she did not ask for her charger."

"You thought Komal stole her phone and her computer, didn't you? But she didn't. She brought them to the man she thought was Marianne's boyfriend. And Mycroft knew that. He also knew Marianne didn't have a boyfriend. So he thought you had sent Marianne for ex-gay therapy. That's why he wouldn't let anyone report her missing. Laura Kwee told Mycroft she had proof that Marianne was having an affair with another woman and she knew some-one who could help her change. At the same time Laura befriended Marianne, telling her she was on her side and wanted to help her."

"I don't understand," Anne Peters said. "We would never have sent Marianne for any kind of corrective therapy. Her health—"

"Marianne had epilepsy," Carla said. "She had to be very careful not to trigger . . . Do you mean she died during ex-gay therapy?"

"But that would not explain what happened to Laura Kwee," Aunty Lee said.

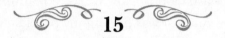

15

At the Hospital

Aunty Lee always maintained that it was impossible to tell how a dish was going to turn out just by reading about how it was made in a recipe. You had to put all the ingredients side by side and prepare them before you could tell how they were going to react with one another. And, of course, there was always the chance that a new ingredient you were unfamiliar with would throw everything else off.

This time the new "ingredient" showed up, not only in the form of a Joseph Cunningham, a tall, gangly, ginger-haired young man (whom Aunty Lee had been expecting and curious to meet), but also in the form of the person he brought with him.

Joseph Cunningham's Singaporean partner, Otto, had arrived at the hospital within an hour after getting Aunty Lee's phone call.

"Actually we were both in Singapore already, before you called, so it wasn't a problem. We were planning our commitment ceremony. I was hoping my parents would fly in, of course, but I didn't know they were already here."

So that was the Cunninghams' big secret, Aunty Lee thought. "How are your parents?"

"Very good considering how things might have turned out. The doctors said to watch out for local infections and cellulitis and it's going to be painful for a while, but with luck they'll be fine in three weeks."

They were talking in Lucy Cunningham's room. Her natural warmth had already broken through her prejudice against gays, and while her son talked to Aunty Lee, Otto was sitting by her bedside listening to her stories about Joe as a child. Now and then she looked over to Joe and Aunty Lee with a big smile on her face. In spite of the angry-looking red-and-white burn blisters visible on her arms and legs (fortunately, she had instinctively blocked her face in time), Lucy Cunningham looked better than Aunty Lee had ever seen her.

"And how is your father taking it?" Aunty Lee asked Joe.

"Do you know why they came to Singapore without telling me? They—or rather my father—wanted to meet up with Otto's parents to try to enlist their help in breaking us up. That was what Laura Kwee was helping them with.

Actually she told them that since same-sex relationships are illegal in Singapore, they could threaten to have Otto arrested if I didn't swear never to see him again. But my mother refused to go along with that. So Laura said she would link them up with Otto's parents if they came out here. She told them that if both sets of parents confronted us together, we would have to give in and they could bring me home. But then she never showed up. Anyway, it wouldn't have worked. Otto's father is dead and his mother totally accepted me. It didn't happen overnight, of course, but she was helping us plan the commitment ceremony. Or rather she's organizing everything."

"Looks like she's going to have some competition . . ."

They both looked across the room as Lucy Cunningham laughed. "What does he mean there are no photographs—I have hundreds, thousands of photographs of my Joe. We can go through them and pick out what you'll use for the montage . . ."

Otto grinned at the others as Joe Cunningham made a wry grimace. This family would go on relatively unscarred, Aunty Lee thought. And she said precisely that.

"I always thought they'd come round," Joe responded. "People who really care find a way to deal with it. Even my dad will, given time. The people who get most upset are those crazies in LifeGifters—you know, the ones who want to save people from being gay? Laura Kwee was involved in it."

"You know Laura Kwee?"

"Never met her. Knew of her. In uni, she had this big crush on Otto. They used to do stuff together. He told her he was gay and thought she was okay with it and supportive, but then she started saying how her father back home kept asking when he was going to marry her and he got scared. Then she started stalking him online and spamming all his friends. She even wrote to the pastor of his church saying he had AIDS after he blocked her on Facebook."

"Why?" Aunty Lee asked.

Joe shrugged. "She thought she was saving him. That's what that LifeGifters network is all about. It's pretty brutal actually. There are stories of how they actually kidnap people to reprogram them for their own good. It's called 'reparative therapy' to supposedly turn gay people straight."

"How does it work?"

Joe looked at Aunty Lee suspiciously but saw only earnest curiosity. "You're locked up and told to pray and read the Bible, particularly verses that cast homosexuality as an abomination. The only people you get to see are those who have given up the 'gay lifestyle.' If you resist, you get tied up and only released to read the Bible and attend church."

"Does it work?"

"Didn't work on me. That's when I told my parents I never wanted to see them again."

"But you invited them to your commitment ceremony."

"I knew they only wanted what was right for me. I wanted to show them I'd found what was right for me."

* * *

Frank Cunningham was alone in his room when Aunty Lee went in. She had brought him some of her brightly colored little cakes, but he only stared at them glumly. Like his wife, his arms and legs were bandaged, and in addition he had a black eye.

"Don't you find it hard to accept people like them?" Frank asked Aunty Lee. "Don't you people have any decency here? It's supposed to be against the law. It's unnatural." But perhaps due to painkillers, he wasn't as vehement as before.

"I believe God gave us brains and logic because He wanted us to learn to use them." Aunty Lee smiled. "We all live by standards that some other people find ridiculous. Laura Kwee was e-mailing you about your son, wasn't she?"

"It was supposed to be confidential. It was for his own good."

"Knock knock!" Harry Sullivan called out, ushering Selina in ahead of him.

"Purely business," Selina said. "Harry says we should come to visit and see how our friends are doing so they don't try to press charges—ha ha! Unless you're already seeing to that, Aunty Lee?"

"Oh no." Aunty Lee waved her hands dismissively. "All over to you. I just came to talk."

"Good. We were just thinking—the shop's been closed for some time now. Customers are going to stop coming. Maybe it would be better to think about closing shop for good and moving on. You're not getting any younger, you know."

Selina was just not very good at the soft approach, Aunty Lee decided. Everything she suggested made Aunty Lee want to head in the opposite direction.

Harry Sullivan stepped in. "Hey, this is not the time, Sel. We just wanted to make sure you folks were okay—you too, Aunty Lee. Not too stressed out from all the traumatic events."

"That's what I said, isn't it?" Selina pointed out.

Harry Sullivan might be balding, paunchy, sweaty, and with damp palms, but these were all physical and therefore superficial details. Still, Aunty Lee wondered whether Selina, in trying to overlook these details, was overlooking too much.

"I just looked in on your wife," Aunty Lee said to Frank. "She's doing well, very well. You know your son's here, don't you?"

"They are sick people. We should be helping them change, not helping them give in to this perversion," Frank said from his bed. "I need more painkillers. Where are the nurses? Where's my wife? She's not as badly hurt as I am. Why can't they send her in to look after me?"

Aunty Lee promised to send a nurse but said no more. This was something Frank Cunningham would have to work out for himself.

As far as Aunty Lee was concerned, people ought to

go through the ideas they carried around in their heads as regularly as they turned out their store cupboards. No matter how wisely you shopped, there would be things in the depths that were past their expiration dates or gone damp and moldy—or that had been picked up on impulse and were no longer relevant. Aunty Lee believed everything inside a head or cupboard could affect everything else in it by going bad or just taking up more space than it was worth.

Harry Sullivan and Selina followed her out of the room. They were talking about claims and insurance. Surely the fire damage hadn't been that extensive?

"I remember it was old Harry Sullivan after all," Lucy Cunningham said when she saw Harry come in. "It's coming back to me now. That's what was on my mind. Harry Sullivan is the name of that old man who had a shop along that row opposite St. Leonards Junction, remember? Across from the old cemetery we went to for your great-granny's hundredth—what would have been her hundredth if she'd made it, and for a while it looked like she was going to. We brought you with us, don't you remember?"

Joe Cunningham did not.

"Your dad got to talking with him. Your old dad can go on forever about his gardening, and the two of them got along wonderfully. We went back to his house to see his precious garden. It was one of the last houses along Park

Road where it joins River Road. A dead-end road and terribly steep, ending in a drop with nothing but a footpath from there down to where they were fixing up River Road. The road was so steep they had frames set into concrete to hold the cars in place. But the garden was spectacular. It must have been under a hundred and fifty square meters, but he had pots and trellises with runner beans and cucumbers. And I saw what I thought were some kind of pumpkin, but they turned out to be the largest tomatoes we ever saw in our lives. He said it was all about the seeds. He insisted on giving Frank some of them, even though Frank said he didn't have the patience to sit around and wait for things to grow. The best seeds from his bull's-heart tomatoes. And they weren't just large. They tasted good!

"He was talking about turning his house into a community garden when he died," she continued. "But then I heard he went so suddenly there was no time. His nephew took care of everything and sold the house."

"How did he die?"

"In his car, strangely enough. One night he got into it and—well, he was an old man and not familiar with driving. He just went straight down and crashed through the barrier at the bottom."

"Why do you say it's strange?" Aunty Lee asked.

"Did I?" Lucy thought about it. "Not strange at all. Just unexpected because he hadn't driven that car for years. He said he didn't even think it still worked, but it cost too much to tow away."

"What's wrong?" Selina asked Harry Sullivan. "Aren't you going to ask her how she is?"

"I think she looks fine," Harry said. He left the room.

"We just need to hear you say you're feeling all right," Selina explained to Lucy before following him. "So that later you can't turn around and sue the café."

"We won't sue you, anyway," Lucy Cunningham said to Aunty Lee. "Not when you've been so kind."

Selina and Harry Sullivan were still in the lobby when Aunty Lee joined them to wait for Nina, who was bringing mushroom barley soup for the invalids.

"Aunty Lee, Harry just told me Laura Kwee was the one writing all those nasty reviews of the café!"

"How did you find out?" Aunty Lee asked him.

"I have contacts," Harry said with an air of mystery. "Of course, I don't mean to speak ill of the dead, but I always suspected something there. Laura could come across a bit strong sometimes. She was either living in her own fantasy dreamworld or she was putting it on to hide something on that computer of hers! Do you know where it is, by the way? I heard it wasn't found at her apartment."

"She probably had it with her. She took it everywhere with her. Laura kept records of everything. She used her phone but backed up everything on her laptop as though she was some kind of secret agent," Selina said, already bored with the talk about Laura. "Laura was the sort to have complicated passwords for the files and then have a list with her passwords because she was also afraid of forgetting. But she kept them in her address book as addresses. That was clever. What was maybe not so clever was her telling people she did it!"

"She didn't have the laptop with her the night she disappeared—I mean the police didn't find it. At least they never said they did," Harry Sullivan persisted. He looked at Aunty Lee. "She didn't leave it at your shop, did she?"

"Nina would know," Aunty Lee said, making a note to warn Nina.

Just then Joe and Otto came out of the room and grabbed Aunty Lee. "We wanted to thank you."

"We're putting together a big family album—digitally," Otto announced. "Joe's going to play it back at the ceremony to show his parents that he did value them and family and everything. He told his mum about his project and she's sending for her huge albums that have been in storage for years."

"It was Otto's idea," Joe said quietly. "I wish I'd thought of it. It made my mum really happy that someone wants to go through all her old photos. If Ots knew all the baggage that came with me . . ." He shook his head.

"Young man, you look at me," Aunty Lee said sternly. "You have so many good men coming after you that you can afford to throw them away?"

"What? No. Of course not."

"Then don't be so stupid. If a Chinese man doesn't want you, you will know. Otherwise the fastest way to drive him away is keep telling him that he should not want to be with you. Chinese men don't like fighting at home. At home they are always very agreeable. One day Otto will agree with you just to get you to stop. Is that what you really want, Joe?"

Joe Cunningham looked blankly at Aunty Lee, almost as though she had been speaking in Mandarin. Then he glanced at Otto.

"I agree," Otto said with a straight face. Aunty Lee found herself liking this young man more and more—she liked both of them in fact, which was nice. Too often, when it came to couples, there would be one she could not stand.

"What?" Now Joe was looking at Otto as though he could not understand him either.

"Look. Would I be marrying you if I didn't want to be with you?"

"I thought I kind of forced you into it. Because I'm insecure and you're nice."

"I'm not that nice. And I love you even though you're not that smart. So just listen to the nice aunty, okay?"

"Thank you, nice Aunty," Joe said obediently. They were all laughing now, Aunty Lee with a touch of exasperation. How could anyone believe in all those theories of evolution if young people today were just as *goondu* as the young people of fifty years ago had been?

"Thank you, Otto," Aunty Lee said. "Now I want to ask you a favor. Will you stay in the hospital for the rest of today at least? You can work here in the waiting room. Show the Cunninghams your photo album. Just stay around here?"

Otto hesitated. "It's not ready. We were going to put in borders and backgrounds and dates and comments and everything."

"Never mind. You can do the fancy work later. I just want you to hang around here for now. Remember, what happened to Frank and Lucy wasn't an accident. The person who attacked them so clumsily this time may do a better job next time."

Nina still had not arrived with the soup. On her way to the ladies', Aunty Lee saw Nina talking to Harry Sullivan in one of the side passages. He was holding her hand—or rather her arm, Aunty Lee saw. He left before Aunty Lee reached them.

"He was not trying to make love to me," Nina said. "He just want me to think so. I can see at once he is acting. I know how to see because I learn from you. Ma'am, he is very angry and very scared."

Nina didn't need to tell Aunty Lee that angry, scared people could be dangerous.

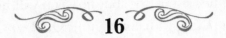

16

Cover and Simmer Over Low Heat

There are times when things need to be done fast. When you are making deep-fried potato curry puffs, for example. You may take your time making your filling—indeed, you have to allow it time to cool before you fold it into its pastry. But once the savory mix of chicken and potato is tucked and folded into its pastry pocket, you have to move quick-quick-quick! The precious pale pastry packages cannot stay in the hot oil a moment longer than it takes to puff them up into all their golden-brown glory. And then again there is no time to waste, because if they are not eaten immediately, the moment of perfection will pass and all you will be left with is a good curry puff. Of course this is not the end of the world. Think of it as falling in love with the most beautiful girl you have ever seen . . . but you cannot have her and you end up with her sister. You would have been happy with your wife if you had not fallen in love with her sister first, but now you will never forget. It is the same thing with curry puffs. Once you have tasted one of Aunty Lee's deep-fried chicken-potato curry puffs freshly fished out of hot oil, no other curry puff will ever satisfy you again.

But then there are also times when moving fast does you no good at all. When making tamarind Assam sauce for instance. You have to let the tamarind paste steep for as long as it takes, moving the mixture around with your fingers to loosen the fibers and seeds . . . so that when you are finally ready to pour the mixture through your metal strainer, you can be sure that all the distractions and irrelevances have been removed while you collect as much of the sauce as possible.

Right now, Aunty Lee thought, she was making tamarind sauce. And she was ready to stick her fingers in to stir.

However, someone else stuck a finger in first . . .

Senior Staff Sergeant Salim turned up at the hospital ward in response to a report that homosexuals were using it as an illegal assembly area to promote the gay lifestyle and that one Nina Balignasay presently there was violating her domestic work contract by working in a shop. SSS Salim thought it strange that the report had come in now, since the shop in question had been closed for a week.

Still, all complaints had to be followed up, and since these violations had occurred under his watch, he decided to follow them up personally—that is, unofficially.

He dismissed the charge of illegal assembly. "You need five people to form an illegal assembly. Unless they are in the vicinity of the Botanic Gardens, where three or more people constitutes an illegal assembly. Two guys visiting a hospital I can't do anything about. But as for the other case—" He looked at Nina doubtfully. "I have to follow up at least. There were dates and times you were seen at the shop working. I must ask you about that."

"Was it that *puti* Harry that made the report that I am working in a shop against regulations for domestic helps?"

"Cannot say, ma'am."

"He only make the report because he came in to seduce me and I say I don't like him," Nina said firmly. "Now he thinks that I will not dare say anything because you will think I am only trying to get revenge on him."

"Did you make a report?" SSS Salim asked. He sounded like a policeman ready to take objective notes. Nina was furious with him.

"You do not believe me? How can you not believe me— you are supposed to help us; instead you come and make trouble for us! Anyway, I told Aunty Lee. Aunty Lee, you tell him to believe me!"

Aunty Lee, frowning in thought, did not hear her at first.

"Aunty Lee! You tell Salim that I told you about Mr. Harry come in here and try to disturb me just now!"

"What? Oh. Yes, she did." Aunty Lee looked vague. "Maybe you should take her in and check her papers."

SSS Salim looked taken aback. Nina was furious. "Ma'am, I am going to be arrested! You are going to be left alone! Please wake up!"

It all had to do, Aunty Lee thought, with Laura Kwee. Everything seemed to lead back to Laura; Laura helping the LifeGifters reform homosexuals, Laura secretly writing articles for *Island High Life* criticizing Aunty Lee's Delights, Laura offering to help Marianne find a private getaway for her and her girlfriend, Laura being a friend to Otto then turning on him and his boyfriend . . .

What had Laura Kwee done to get herself killed? She had a pattern of falling for unsuitable men and believing that making herself the "right" kind of woman would win them over. She had tried to win Otto over; probably Mark too. Had Laura thought Mark would leave Selina for her because she slept with him once when he and Selina were going through a bad patch? Had Selina thought he might? Aunty Lee suspected it had been Selina who kept Laura Kwee around. To punish Mark perhaps? And to keep an eye on Laura? Whether he knew it or not, Mark never did anything Selina did not approve of. When she was tipsy at the first wine dining, Laura had been flirting with Mark and Harry Sullivan. After the second wine dining, even though she had hardly drunk anything, Laura had seemed even more drunk than she had been the first time . . . and she had been teasing Harry Sullivan about

Marianne Peters, Aunty Lee remembered. It was a good thing Marianne had not been there that night. Laura had brought cupcakes—including a matching pair of "engagement cupcakes," as she insisted on calling them, for Harry and Marianne—she had made and iced herself.

Cherril Lim-Peters had thought Laura was trying to blackmail Harry with her hints and allusions, but that was just Laura's way of flirting. Still, if they sounded like blackmail threats to Cherril, they might have sounded that way to Harry too.

Aunty Lee was pulled abruptly back into the present by the altercation that was going on.

"I will take down your statement," Salim said smoothly. "But that is a separate matter. I still have to follow up on his complaint. Are you here on a domestic helper visa?"

"No, I am here on a 'secret mission to marry a rich man and steal all his money to go back to the Philippines' visa!"

"I don't think Nina means that," Aunty Lee said, suddenly aware that Nina might be talking herself into more trouble than was good for her.

"That's a 'yes,' right?" Salim was still being professional. Nina wanted to hit him with something. If challenged, she would say she was just trying to knock his skull hard enough to wake him up. "And you are employing her to be a companion to you, ma'am?" This was directed to Aunty Lee.

"Oh yes. Yes, she is."

"So, as a companion to you, Nina has to go wherever you are going to look after you?"

"Yes."

"For example, she spends much of her time in the shop?"

Just as Nina thought things were sorting themselves out, Aunty Lee said, "Maybe you should take Nina to the station with you to talk things over."

SSS Salim looked as taken aback as Nina. "Sorry?"

"Ma'am!" Nina said. "What are you doing? I cannot leave you alone here!"

"I will talk to you on the phone. Call me once you get there."

"But how are you going to get home?" Nina knew Aunty Lee was perfectly capable of giving her address to a taxi driver, but it had been a long time since she had taken a cab alone.

"Selina will help me I'm sure."

"Ma'am, Selina is gone home already!"

"Has she? Oh no—look. Here she is."

"What's happening?" Selina joined them to ask. "Is something wrong?"

The way she said this suggested she knew exactly what was wrong. Nina allowed herself to be led away by SSS Salim. She had learned to trust Aunty Lee's sudden eccentric decisions, but what if this last action was prompted by her feeling that she no longer needed Nina? Well then—if that was the case, Nina thought, there was no reason for her to worry about Aunty Lee! She stepped into the lift as SSS Salim held the door open for her.

"Wait, wait, wait."

Nina turned around hopefully while SSS Salim girded himself for further changes in plan.

They were both taken aback when Aunty Lee asked him, "Was there ash on top of the phone? When your men found it in the bin. How much cigarette ash was on top of the phone? And was all the ash from the same cigarettes? Those people always checking on how much nicotine and how much tar should be able to tell you."

Senior Staff Sergeant Salim was jerked to attention when he arrived back at the station with a sullen Nina—it had been a long drive and he was hoping the money plant on his desk was still alive. If it had not survived, he would have to replace it rather than tell Nina he could not keep something as easy to care for as a money plant alive. Or perhaps he would bring Nina to see the HortPark, she would like that—then suddenly he was back at the police post and an overexcited Officer Pang was banging on the driver's-side window of the car.

"Sir! Sir! Sir!" Officer Pang shouted, grinning.

"What?" As one who had survived and conquered National Service and academic life, Salim had long ago mastered the art of instantly waking to his full senses.

"What is it?"

"Sir! Harry Sullivan is dead!"

It was not the young man's words but his obvious delight

that SSS Salim found confusing. "I see," he said neutrally. He felt grimy and slightly guilty for dreaming about Nina instead of focusing on the case.

"According to this report, Harry Sullivan died seven years ago, sir."

"That's the other Harry Sullivan. The Cunninghams' old friend. We already know about him."

"Yes, sir. And according to the records from the passports and immigration department, that is the Harry Sullivan who came into Singapore six months ago. Same date of birth at the same place. Passport applied for from the same residential address in St. Leonards, Sydney."

"You sure about this?"

"Absolutely totally certain, sir!"

Timothy Pang's long-lashed brown eyes beneath the head of close-cut dark hair stared at his senior officer eagerly. He was almost trembling with excitement and hope of being in on the arrest—if he had had a tail, he would have wagged it. SSS Salim wondered if he himself had ever been so young and so eager. If he had, he was already too old to remember it.

"Good work," Salim said to the still-beaming Officer Pang. "Anything else?"

"Harry Sullivan's death was registered by his sister's son—one Sam Ekkers. Mr. Ekkers failed to inform the pensions department, which continued forwarding Harry Sullivan's pension checks care of Sam Ekkers. A Sentosa beachfront chalet in the area you outlined was booked under the name of Sam Ekkers. We talked to staff there—I have their statements."

SSS Salim looked at Officer Pang's report. The chalet had been booked under the name of Sam Ekkers for two weeks. He had declined all housekeeping services and been seen there with two different women. The staff had not seen anything unusual in this, being used to rich, foreign visitors.

Nina, ignoring him, remained seated in the car. She also ignored Officer Pang. Meanwhile, something suddenly clicked in place for SSS Salim and he found he no longer resented Officer Pang's youthful good looks or anything else.

"Come on," he said to Nina, who looked surprised at the sudden energy in his voice. "We better go call your boss. Let's go see whether we can find what this Mr. Harry Sullivan is up to."

17

Making Tea

Making tea is a more precise business than anyone brought up on tea bags can imagine. But at the same time it is very forgiving.

"Excuse me."

The storeroom door opened and suddenly Aunty Lee was standing there peering into the room, in her affable but shortsighted way. "Nina's not with me right now and I'm having a bit of trouble managing. My eyes are not so good anymore. If you're not too busy, Selina, I was hoping you would come and give me a hand in the shop . . ."

Selina suddenly felt like laughing. Or perhaps crying. She was feeling so sleepy at the moment that she wasn't sure there was a difference between the two.

When Harry Sullivan and Selina Lee arrived at Aunty Lee's Delights, it was dark and closed up. Selina had had to use her key to let them in and they had thought no one was there. Harry had gotten them drinks and was looking around the place. He had been just about to open the storeroom door when Aunty Lee opened it from the inside.

"Harry Sullivan wanted to visit the café when you were not here," Selina explained lamely. "He knows someone who is interested in buying us out. It could be the best thing for us, given how things are going."

"Sorry, I'm running a sinking ship today. Everything is upside down. I don't know what I'm doing. I'm sorry, if you want coffee or a cold drink, I'll get it for you, but I won't be serving any food. I have to go and see what's happening to Nina. I told them I had to just lock up the shop here. I phoned Mark and told him to go straight to the ministry. There must be somebody who can help. I need Nina!"

"What happened?" Harry Sullivan could see that the old woman was upset. His voice was calm and soothing as he pulled out a chair for her. "Come and sit down, Mrs. Lee. Join us in a drink . . . sounds so upside down, right? Me offering you a drink here?"

"No, no. I'm all right. Let me get you both something to drink. Give me something to do. Do you really think I should close the shop?"

Harry Sullivan was looking along the shelves. "Any idea when Nina will be back?"

Aunty Lee shook her head. Clearly she did not expect her employee back anytime soon. "Don't know whether she's coming back at all. I don't know what's going to happen. I can't carry on without her."

"Any idea where Nina would put things that people left behind here?"

Selina snorted. "She would probably keep them. You should see some of the things she has!" Having said this, she put her head down on the table and promptly fell asleep.

Aunty Lee looked at her.

"It's been a long day," Harry Sullivan said. He pushed a cup toward Aunty Lee. "Have a drink. I'm sure you'll hear from Nina soon."

"Nina will be fine. At worst, they'll send her back home, and by now she should be the richest person in her village if her family hasn't spent all the money I paid her. You should ask what's going to happen to me! Any person who illegally employs or abets the illegal employment of foreigners may face a fine of up to fifteen thousand dollars, or be jailed up to twelve months, or both. I'm the one that's going to end up in prison."

As he watched Aunty Lee take a sip of her tea, Harry Sullivan drank some more himself. He was suddenly feeling very thirsty and poured himself another cup from the hideous yellow-flowered teapot.

"More for you? But maybe we shouldn't dilute the stuff."

He saw Aunty Lee's cup was still almost full. "We'll wait till you've finished, shall we?"

"You didn't mean to kill your uncle, did you?" Aunty Lee said to Harry Sullivan conversationally.

"What are you talking about?"

"The real Harry Sullivan. Or rather I should say the original Harry Sullivan. Because as far as we are concerned here in Singapore, you came in on the real Harry Sullivan's passport, right? Where was I . . . oh yes, your uncle. I was just saying I don't believe you meant to kill your uncle Harry Sullivan." There was no accusation in her voice— nothing more than vague curiosity. Aunty Lee sounded as though she were trying to pin down a memory about an old friend or place. She looked hopefully at Harry Sullivan as though he was the only one who could supply her with an answer.

"I didn't kill him," Harry said heavily. Suddenly it was very important to him to set the record straight. "He just dropped dead. Didn't even drop, as a matter of fact. Just sat at the table being dead. And right after I got there too. You can't count on family these days. The old bugger never so much as sent us a Christmas pressie all these years, and when we show up, what does he do but drop dead!"

"So you put him in his car," Aunty Lee prompted. As Harry Sullivan watched, she took an encouraging sip of her tea. That was good. He had to keep her drinking, keep talking to her to distract her.

"I put him in his old car. Car was as dead as he was.

Useless. All useless—the old man, the old car, that falling-apart old shack he called a house. At least I was giving him a burial at sea, so to speak."

"And then you helped yourself to his things. His name, his papers, his pension . . ."

"Old fart wasn't going to need them where he was headed, was he? Besides, there were no other relations left for him to leave anything to. If there were, they would have been my relatives too, wouldn't they? They'd have some obligation to keep an eye out for a relative in desperate need, wouldn't they? But, oh no. Nobody qualified as a relative, I tell you! I wouldn't have them if they held a gun to my head!"

Aunty Lee nodded as though this made perfect sense to her. "We can't choose our relatives," she agreed. She poured out more tea for them both. Her hand seemed quite steady. Harry wondered whether too much tea would dilute the effects.

"You didn't mean to kill Marianne Peters either, did you?"

"I didn't kill Marianne! You see, I knew that's what people like you would think. Everything's my fault. Let's pick on someone to blame, someone who nobody is ever going to listen to or believe. We'll put the blame on him and string him up for it, why not. Why bother to find out what really happened? Who cares what really happened! I knew it. I knew that's how it was going to come down."

"Did you know poor Marianne had epilepsy?" Aunty

Lee said. "Not many people knew. She looked so normal, didn't she? And then when she had a seizure—" Aunty Lee closed her eyes and shuddered slightly, as though at a horrible memory.

"Exactly!" He thumped the table, knocking his teacup over. "She was rolling her eyes and shaking. It was like something out of *The Exorcist*. Scared me shitless. I tried to get her to stop. Tried splashing her with water—like for shock, but she wouldn't stop."

"Did you call for an ambulance?"

"I thought I'd wait. Just see whether she stopped on her own, you know. I thought she would. But when I went back—well, she was already dead, so there was no point."

"You left her alone? For how long?"

"You know for how long." He was getting tired. All these women were so stupid. "I came for the wine dining that night, remember? That was the night Miss Laura decided to surprise us all with her bloody cupcakes after the dinner. If it hadn't been for her, I would have got back to Marianne earlier. I might have been able to do something to help her, the poor girl. It's all that stupid slut bitch's fault that Marianne died. The way she was going on and on about her cupcakes as a bloody art form. If you're looking for someone to blame for what happened to poor Marianne, you put the blame on that one!"

"Only it's no use blaming Laura Kwee now, is it?" Aunty Lee stood up, pushing her chair away from the table.

He looked at her blearily. There was something wrong

but his sluggish brain could not pinpoint what it was. His body was quite comfortable where it was—though it would have felt good to lie down. Or he could put his head down on the table and nap right there like Selina was doing. The tea-wet surface of the table suddenly looked very inviting.

"Feeling tired?"

"Yeah. Don't you?" He knew the old woman should have been the one lying unconscious on the floor, but she was still pottering around. Once she fell asleep, he would find Laura Kwee's laptop and get himself out of there for good.

"It's the tea," Aunty Lee said from a great distance. "If you drink the right tea, it gives you energy."

He looked at his spilled tea. It had pooled on the table in an oval shape without trickling off. The tabletop was perfectly level. It looked like something one of those modern artists would put up as a work of art. Normally he would have snorted at the thought, but suddenly, as he looked at the clear, thin golden-brown liquid, it looked beautiful to him. And he was awfully sleepy.

"Why did you kill Laura Kwee?" Aunty Lee asked him sharply.

He had to search his brain to remember who she was talking about.

"She was a bitch."

Aunty Lee nodded agreeably. She had brought a bowl and a round, wooden chopping board back to the table. "Perhaps. But why did you kill her?"

"It's none of your fucking business." He would go to

sleep for a while, he decided. Then, when he woke up, he would kill this old woman who was standing in front of him taking things out of her bowl and putting them onto the chopping board. He told her so. "Because she's just like you. Fucking busybody bitches. What are you doing?"

"Pig's foot," Aunty Lee said sweetly. "You want to know what human beings taste like, all you have to do is eat pork." She lifted a chopper and expertly whacked the long, pale-skinned leg. "Very sweet. You and the pig are both red meat. Your muscles about the same size. You eat your junk food, the pig eats what is left over from making your junk food, so same taste, same texture, only difference is your meat is juicier."

He stared at her blearily, trying to work out what she was saying.

Aunty Lee brought her chopper down and cleanly dismembered a section of the pig's foot. "I tell you, most people cannot tell the difference whether they are eating pig meat or human meat—" She peered at the meat through her spectacles, poked at something, then reached for an enormous pair of tweezers. "Nina is supposed to pull out all the hair for me first. But sometimes they are extra hairy—like you. Look at your hands!"

"Nothing wrong with my hands." He stretched out his hands and looked at his good strong fingers with their curly ginger hair.

"Do you know how long it would take me to get all that

hair off your fingers?" The thwack of Aunty Lee's chopper startled him. "Same like people's hands, you see—"
Thwack. "If you chop at the right place, you can cut up the fingers clean through. No chips. People don't like to bite into bits of bone. But very hard to teach people to chop nowadays. Hard to get fresh meat to practice on—"

He curled his fingers protectively in his palms as Aunty Lee thwacked again.

"Why did you kill Laura Kwee?" she asked again, holding up the chopper.

"You're mad," he said. He tried to get up, but his legs seemed strangely detached from the rest of his body.

"You don't need to be very strong. You don't even need a very sharp knife as long as you know where to chop."

"She's the one that was coming after me," he whined. "I didn't want to have anything to do with her."

Aunty Lee came around the table and moved toward him, nonchalantly hefting her chopper. She picked up one of his limp hands and shook it as he watched helplessly.

"Really? What happened?"

"She was trying to blackmail me. She was saying how she saw me and Marianne together, how well we got along. She kept asking if Marianne told me where she was going. I know her type. She was trying to scare me out of everything I had, then after that, she would have sold me out. I know her type! I was only trying to stop her, that's all. It was self-defense!" He could barely speak, but what was left of his conscious brain told him to say whatever he had to in order to get this madwoman away from him.

Just then, SSS Salim, Nina, and Carla Saito appeared from the inner pantry, Nina flying to Aunty Lee's side so fast that Aunty Lee almost did not notice the quick, grateful look she gave the police officer. "Ma'am! Can already!"

"Did you get it?" Aunty Lee asked. "Can you use it as evidence? Can you make copies?"

"I can but I won't," Carla Saito said. "I've already put it on YouTube. The police can get it from there."

"She insisted on coming," SSS Salim explained. "Are you all right, Mrs. Lee?"

"I'm not all right!" Harry Sullivan moaned. "She put something in my tea, she drugged me. I could be dying—do something!"

"What did you put in his tea?" SSS Salim asked Aunty Lee.

Aunty Lee shook her head in innocent wonder. "Tea— *pu erh*—but I added some licorice bark and some fennel seeds and some dragon-eye berries . . . I know it's an unusal combination, but he was looking a bit under stress and I was feeling sleepy myself, so I thought—"

"She's lying!" the man wailed wetly. "Make her tell you what she put in my tea!"

"I may have accidentally switched our cups," Aunty Lee said steadily. "Maybe you should ask him what he put into my cup?"

Harry Sullivan moaned.

"I didn't mean to," Harry Sullivan said. "It was all a terrible accident, a terrible mistake. I'm not a murderer."

"So you accidentally tried to put poison in my tea?" Aunty Lee said, as though trying to understand his point of view. "Luckily my tea counteracts the effects. You should be grateful you did not get as big a dose as you gave those poor girls. You drugged them like you drugged Selina, didn't you? Laura Kwee wasn't drunk that night. She was sitting next to you, you slipped something into her cup."

Harry Sullivan stared blearily at Carla Saito. "If you hadn't come to Singapore, everything would have been fine."

"Here. Make him drink this."

"What is it?" Salim hesitated.

"Mustard and water. He'll get over the effects faster. And hold him over that basin. It's all going to come up. Better now than later. Did you call your people to come and collect him yet?"

"On their way."

"Good," Aunty Lee said, then to Harry, "Drink up, then. Better get it out of your system now rather than in the police car."

Aunty Lee went on with her chopping and tweezing as Harry Sullivan purged himself.

Harry Sullivan tried to bluster. "She was threatening me. I have my rights. I want my lawyer. You can't hold me. I thought I was dying. Of course I said whatever she wanted!"

This last was directed at SSS Salim, who only looked at

him curiously before asking Aunty Lee, "What about Mrs. Selina Lee?"

"I think we'll let her sleep it off."

"According to his documents, Harry Sullivan would be eighty years old now. Immigration didn't notice. They must have just glanced at the younger Harry, at the photo. Probably assumed it was a bad photo and didn't bother noticing the age." Anyway, age was so difficult to tell with Caucasians. They liked to sit in the sun and make their skin look older.

"I believe he didn't mean to kill Marianne. He took her over to Sentosa to see the cabin he booked. I suppose that's the cabin you told her you would let her have for a week or two. Only she didn't want to stay in it with you, did she?"

"I was only trying to help her," Harry Sullivan said. "Look, Officer, man-to-man, you can see that. I was trying to give her a chance, help her change. Even her family would have seen it would be good for her to be with a real man."

"Let me kill him." Carla Saito started toward him. "You can hang me after. It'll be worth it—"

"And Laura Kwee?" Aunty Lee asked calmly.

"Laura Kwee—she knew about Sentosa. She kept going on about the Sentosa cabin, how 'fun' it must be, how she just wanted to see it. In the end I just brought her over and gave her what she wanted."

"Laura was flirting with you, you know. That's how she flirted. She just wasn't very good at it."

Aunty Lee finished chopping her pig's foot with a last satisfying thwack. "Fingers," she said. "If you slice through the joints, no chips."

Salim would not be the only one not eating pork for a while.

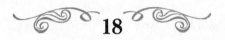

18

Aunty Lee's Wrap-up

One of Aunty Lee's Delights' greatest catering successes was the commitment celebration of Otto Thio and Joseph Cunningham on the Sentosa beachfront not far from where everything began. As Aunty Lee always said, you can't cut out bad memories without removing part of your heart, but you can always create good memories to override them.

Harry Sullivan—or Sam Ekkers, as he was really named—was charged in Singapore with the murders of Marianne Peters and Laura Kwee. This triggered an extradition stalemate because according to the records, Sam Ekkers had never entered Singapore, Harry Sullivan was dead in Australia, and these nations held different views on the death penalty.

But as far as Aunty Lee was concerned, the case was over. The man would not be hurting any more women. She went to watch *The Bodies on Sentosa,* a local musical based on the events of the case and written by Joe Cunningham's husband, Otto, which opened at the Esplanade Theater. The show was a great success, but it was overshadowed (in Aunty Lee's opinion) by the incredible food at the show's opening night party—catered by Aunty Lee's Delights.

Acknowledgments

Special thanks to the wonderful people at William Morrow: associate publisher and marketing director Jen Hart, creative director Mary Schuck (who created the lovely jacket), marketing coordinator Alaina Waagner, production editor Joyce Wong, publicist Joanne Minutillo, international sales directors Samantha Hagerbaumer and Christine Swedowsky, and especially to my editor Rachel Kahan and assistant editor Trish Daly. Big thanks also to Jayapriya Vasudevan, Priya Doraswamy, and Helen Mangham, my cheerleaders/coaches/agents from Books@Jacaranda.

With them doing the real work, I had fun writing and any faults in the book are mine alone.

Aunty Lee's Amazing Achar
(easy home version)

Singapore *achar* is a sweet and spicy vegetable pickle eaten with everything from hot curries to plain rice and even bread and butter. Some commonly used ingredients include sambal belachan, blue ginger, lemongrass, home-dried limes, and tamarind pulp, but the point is really to use whatever you have on hand!

Prepare at least a day in advance. The longer it stays in your fridge the better it will taste.

Ingredients:

2 cups vegetables, chopped into thick matchsticks and bite-sized morsels. Use what you have and more of what you like. Traditional vegetables include cucumbers, carrots, Napa cabbage, red onions, hot peppers, cauliflower, and green beans. Leave the skin on the cucumbers and carrots but remove the seeds from cucumbers and hot peppers. For crunchier pickles rub a tablespoon of salt into your cucumber sticks and leave them to sweat.

Blanching Solution:
   ½ cup your best vinegar (can be white vinegar, rice vinegar, or
      wine vinegar. Remember: the better the vinegar the better
      your pickles!)
   ½ cup water
   1 teaspoon salt
   1 teaspoon sugar

For Rempah (Spice Paste):
   1 red onion (chopped)
   1 clove garlic
   1 nub fresh ginger
   1 nub fresh turmeric
   2 dried hot peppers

1 tablespoon toasted belachan (fermented shrimp
　　paste) Or use 1 teaspoon each of ginger and turmeric
　　powder and 1 tablespoon of red chili pepper flakes,
　　and substitute 1 tablespoon of anchovy paste for the
　　belachan.

Final Touch Ingredients:
½ cup vinegar (see above)
Fresh juice of one large lime (or half a lemon)
Dash of salt and pepper
Small can of pineapple chunks
Crushed roasted peanuts
Toasted sesame seeds

How to Prepare:
Turn on your radio or television and turn off your phone.

Bring your blanching solution to a boil. Blanch all your chopped vegetables (except for the cucumbers) and lay them out to dry on kitchen towels, where the cucumbers can rejoin them. The more you dry them here the better they will absorb your marinade later.

Blend all your rempah ingredients into a paste. If using powders you may need a few drops of oil to bind them. Heat a pan with a little oil and stir-fry your spice paste over low heat until it smells good. This will take 10 to 15 minutes.

Add ½ cup vinegar, the lime juice, and a teaspoon each of salt and sugar. Bring the mixture to a boil then remove from heat immediately.

In a glass or ceramic bowl, add your pineapple chunks, peanuts, sesame seeds, and all your vegetables and mix well, pressing them down in the bowl. The marinade won't cover the vegetables at this stage but the level will rise as your vegetables pickle.

If not eaten immediately, your *achar* should be stored in a glass container in the fridge. Stir thoroughly each time you help yourself.

About the author

About the book

Insights,
Interviews
& More...

Meet Ovidia Yu

OVIDIA YU is one of Singapore's best-known and most acclaimed writers. Since dropping out of medical school to write for the theater, she has had more than thirty plays produced in Singapore, Malaysia, Australia, the United Kingdom, and the United States, including the Edinburgh Fringe First Award–winning play *The Woman in a Tree on the Hill.*

The author of a number of mysteries that have been published in Singapore and India, Ovidia Yu received a Fulbright Fellowship to attend the University of Iowa's International Writers Program, and has been a writing fellow at the National University of Singapore. She speaks frequently at literary festivals and writers' conferences throughout Asia.

Despite her writing career, when she is recognized in Singapore it is usually because of her stint as a regular celebrity guest on Singapore's version of the American television game show *Pyramid.* ◠

Kar-Wai Wesley

A Conversation Between Ovidia Yu and Louise Penny

Louise Penny: *You've outed yourself as a lifelong Agatha Christie fan—does Rosie Lee owe her existence to Miss Marple, or any of Agatha Christie's other sleuthing heroines?*

Ovidia Yu: I'm sure she does, not directly as an "old-lady detective" figure, but because I owe my existence as it is to Agatha Christie's books. It was through her books that I first fell in love with reading, and I thought I was in love with the world she set her books in. For a long time I thought that "world" was English country villages . . . in the '50s and gone forever. But then I got that same feeling—that people in terrible situations struggling to solve real problems were in spite of everything still trying to be human and good— from your books (sorry to drag you in— just in this one answer, I promise!) and realized it was a way of seeing the world that wasn't found only in vintage England. That you could create that same magic in books set in contemporary Canada gave me "permission" (which I had not realized I'd been denying myself!) to write about Singapore. Actually, my lightbulb moment didn't happen till after you visited Singapore with your husband. You were the first real-life writer I'd met—till then I'd thought some pact ▶

A Conversation Between Ovidia Yu and Louise Penny *(continued)*

with the devil was necessary to succeed in writing; but I saw that you were as in love with life as with writing, and that's when I decided to allow myself to write what I wanted to read—set in Singapore.

But to get back to Agatha Christie very quickly, Miss Marple isn't my favorite lady sleuth. I think that would be a tie between Henrietta Savernake (*The Hollow*) and Lucy Eyelesbarrow (*4:50 from Paddington*). Henrietta is the artist I would love to be, or, failing that, love to create. She's good with people, intelligent, artistic, knits well, and survives heartbreak: "Grief, in alabaster" . . . diehard Christie fans will know what I mean. Carla Saito owes something to her, I think. And Lucy Eyelesbarrow, who cooks fantastically, works for a living but sets aside private time for herself and solves mysteries with practical humor—I like to think Aunty Lee owes something of her genesis to Lucy Eyelesbarrow!

LP: *Thank you! Like Rosie Lee, you're a native-born Singaporean and also Peranakan. Can you explain Peranakan culture to readers who might not have heard of it? Is Aunty Lee a typical Peranakan lady, or something of an iconoclast in her community?*

OY: Oh dear—I'm not a true Peranakan. My late mother was Shanghainese, not Straits born, but in Singapore once you accept yourself as Singaporean, that means having access to all the cultures here. Aunty Lee is a typical "Peranakan Aunty" because like so many of them (whether truly Peranakan or not) she is a great cook and very good at running her own business as well as everyone else's. Peranakan aunties have very strong practical streaks and very strong wills. But they can also be flamboyant, funny, and fond of luxury.

LP: *Singapore has a reputation for being almost fantastically clean, well-run, cosmopolitan, and tourist-friendly. Are there hidden depths to its glossy exterior?*

OY: I hope so! Singapore reminds me of the house I grew up in. My parents had a carefully maintained foyer and lounge for visitors—designed to look good and be easy to clean—but our real "living" took place elsewhere, in the playroom or out back where there were rabbits and chickens. Singapore is a very, very small place and for those of us who live here it sometimes feels like it is getting smaller and smaller. But the clean, well-run side of things is the schoolroom side. The teachers running the schoolroom are a bit authoritarian at times, but I think as we grow up as a country and earn their trust, they will ease up on what is allowed and we'll be able to draw on the roots in the "hidden depths" and grow wider and wilder branches in unhidden heights! Yes, there's the side of us that's ▸

A Conversation Between Ovidia Yu and Louise Penny *(continued)*

clean, competitive, and cosmopolitan, but that's just our on-show side.

LP: *Aunty Lee's secret weapon seems to be her home cooking; is this based on your own love of cooking, or do you know aunties like her?*

OY: Sadly, I am a survival cook. But that just makes me love people who can cook all the more, and, yes, there are many, many "cooking aunties" in Singapore. My Aunty Lian, for example, is (in my humble opinion) one of the best cooks alive and single-handedly maintains harmonious family relationships thanks to her hosting of family dinners! As someone who loves to eat I'd say I owe these cooking aunties a lot. It's not just the food they put on the table but all the preparation (and, yes, they will be only too happy to tell you about it!) that goes into it. If you want to test this, the next time you are in Singapore in the vicinity of a genuine Peranakan aunty, ask her how she prepares her Buah Keluak (Buah Keluak are a type of nut that are difficult to eat as well as to prepare, so you'll have lots of time to listen to her answer). She will probably start talking about symptoms of cyanide poisoning and ash and banana leaves, and you'll see how naturally the conjunction of cooking and murder occurs. But I love these nuts. They grow in mangrove swamps and are eaten by wild pigs but are poisonous to humans unless prepared perfectly. Sadly, Singapore has few mangrove swamps left and even fewer wild pigs, so I believe most of our nuts come from Indonesia now.

LP: *As a writer, I know that inspiration can come from many different places: a quote, a childhood experience—the sky is the limit. What inspired you to write this novel?*

OY: Actually, I started by wanting to write about Sentosa. People know Sentosa as a tourist attraction today, but it used to be called "Pulau Blakang Mati," or island of unexpected death. When I was young we would spend our school holidays on these small offshore islands and I loved them. Much as I appreciate clean water and good sanitation, part of me misses the atmosphere of the old days. Remains of bodies thrown into the sea by the Japanese during the war used to wash up on Sentosa and that's where I put the first murder victim in the book . . . everything else followed from there.

LP: *You set your novel in Singapore— do you think it will resonate with contemporary American audiences?*

OY: It didn't occur to me till now that it might not, but I think we'll have to wait and see! Contemporary America is such a big part of Singapore life because of television, movies, and, of course, the ▶

A Conversation Between Ovidia Yu and Louise Penny *(continued)*

Internet that it's easy to forget how different things here might appear to people in America. But having said that, most of the American visitors I've met here seem to adapt to Singapore quite easily. I think because we're English-speaking, they find us a good, safe spot from which to kick off an exploration of Asia. And I hope my writing will act as an introduction to Singapore and Asia too!

LP: *Can you explain the connection between a rather strict, safe country and delight in reading about murders?*

OY: I think we read to learn about ourselves as well as to escape from our everyday lives and for entertainment. I love reading murder stories. But if I were living in a dangerous place with murders happening on my street I don't think I would—I would probably be reading Rumi!

LP: *You've written several well-received plays. What inspired you to write a novel?*

OY: A whole bunch of things actually. I've always loved reading novels, especially mysteries. But all the books I loved most were written by people who lived in England or America about people who lived in England or America, and without thinking about it I assumed it was out of reach for me. Then I joined an online group based on Julia Cameron's book *The Artist's Way* and I read some of Wayne Dyer's books (which bizarrely made me return to Asian classic guides I had rejected while growing up) and I realized that instead of spending my life preparing to write books I should just start. And then I found the NaNoWriMo (National Novel Writing Month) and wrote the first draft of *Aunty Lee's Delights* in a month. At that time it was titled *The Body on Sentosa*. It helped having so much online support because writing a play you get "support" from your director, your actors ("write me a part that I can play without losing weight but without calling me fat!"), and your producer ("we need a casting script by tomorrow and we can't move the pipe organ out so write it in"), so compared to that writing every day on my own felt like a very lonely business.

LP: *On page 162 of* Aunty Lee's Delights, *Aunty Lee says, "I feel responsible for the people I feed. Once my food has gone into them and become part of them and their lives, I become part of their lives. In a way I love them." Do you believe that is true?*

OY: I believe that in a way we're responsible to everyone who crosses our path. Either we can learn something from them or do something to help them, and just enjoying the meeting ▶

A Conversation Between Ovidia Yu and Louise Penny *(continued)*

makes it a good encounter. If you're like Aunty Lee and you nurture people with food, then it is true for you. I would certainly like it to be true of me, though only if I can find a way to feed people through my writing, because that would be safer for all concerned!

LP: Aunty Lee's Delights *deals with visitors from Australia and America as well as ethnic Chinese, Indian, Malay, Eurasian, and Filipino residents. Was this an effort to reach out to an international audience?*

OY: Actually, that's just how we are in Singapore. Here in my apartment block my neighbors are Chinese-speaking, and across the lobby there's a German family and a Czech couple. But for Lunar New Year the Germans put up decorations and gave out good luck oranges like the Chinese, and the Czechs went on a getaway to Thailand like many Singaporeans, and my Chinese (though not Peranakan) aunty neighbor spent days cooking and fed us all on the results! I think because we are a nation of immigrants it's both easier for outsiders to find a place here and harder for Singaporeans to define who and what we are. The main effort I'm making here is to figure out who we are—writing is my favorite way of working things out—but I want to figure that out for myself rather than for an audience! ᴄ◠

Reading Group Guide

1. When her wealthy husband died, Rosie Lee could have settled for life as a Tai-Tai: "wearing designer clothes and going for manicures and overseas holidays." Why do you think she decided to open Aunty Lee's Delights instead?

2. How would you describe Aunty Lee's relationship with her stepson, Mark, and his wife, Selina? What's her motive for keeping them close? And what is theirs for staying close?

3. "To Aunty Lee, comfort meant being dressed for the job. It was obvious to her that getting the upper hand in an interview with a police officer required a different outfit from supervising the cleaning of bean sprouts." What do you think of Aunty Lee's deliberate change of clothing? Do we tend to change how we present ourselves depending on who we're dealing with?

4. How women dress is frequently commented upon in *Aunty Lee's Delights*, from Aunty Lee's changes of clothing to Selina's belief that "how women talked, dressed, and behaved was to blame for unwanted male attention" to Frank Cunningham's proclamation that "short-haired women in pants . . . it's just not right." How do these views reveal things about the characters who hold them? How do the different women in the novel— ▶

Selina, Carla, and Nina, for example—deal with expectations about how they should look and behave?

5. When Aunty Lee goes to visit SSS Salim at his office, she makes sure to take along an assortment of her best snacks, which are so delicious that the previously wary Salim "looked across at Aunty Lee with something like devotion in his eyes." Give other examples of Aunty Lee using her culinary powers to influence people. Is there a special food guaranteed to earn your devotion?

6. Aunty Lee says that she is personally invested in finding Laura and Marianne's killer because "The two girls who died both came to eat in my restaurant. If they ate my cooking, they are my guests and they are my family." Later she tells Carla, "I feel responsible for the people I feed. Once my food has gone into them and become part of them and their lives, I become part of their lives." Do you believe her? Are there other reasons for her sleuthing?

7. The characters in *Aunty Lee's Delights* come from the many ethnic communities who live in Singapore, including Indian, Australian, Filipino, and Peranakan (people of mixed Malay and Chinese descent like Aunty Lee and the novel's author, Ovidia Yu). Do the

characters still fit into a kind of social hierarchy, or are they all treated equally in Singaporean culture? Can you detect positives and negatives about this mix of ethnicities?

8. Aunty Lee reflects that "People ought to go through the ideas they carried around in their heads regularly as they turned out their store cupboards. No matter how wisely you shopped, there would be things in the depths that were past their expiration dates or gone damp and moldy—or that had been picked up on impulse and were no longer relevant. Aunty Lee believed everything inside a head or cupboard could affect everything else in it by going bad, or just taking up more space than it was worth." Which characters have ideas that might need to be updated or discarded? Which have a few bad ideas that might be spoiling everything else in their lives?

9. Rosie Lee's late husband, M. L. Lee, described her as "*em zhai se*—not afraid to die," which describes how "Aunty Lee drove everyone around her through frustration to despair as she pursued some triviality that no one else could see any point in." What do you make of this description of Aunty Lee? By the end of the novel, how has her *em zhai se* personality made a difference?